A King Production presents…

Last Bitch Standing

A Novel

DEJA KING

This novel is a work of fiction. Any references to real people, events, establishments, or locales are intended only to give the fiction a sense of reality and authenticity. Other names, characters, and incidents occurring in the work are either the product of the author's imagination or are used fictitiously, as those fictionalized events and incidents that involve real persons. Any character that happens to share the name of a person who is an acquaintance of the author, past or present, is purely coincidental and is in no way intended to be an actual account involving that person.

ISBN 10: 097558118X
ISBN 13: 978-0975581186
Cover concept by Deja King & www.MarionDesigns.com
Cover model: Deja King
Cover layout and graphic design by: www.MarionDesigns.com
Typesetting: Marion Designs
Editor: Linda Williams and Dolly Lopez

Library of Congress Cataloging-in-Publication Data;
King, Joy

Last Bitch Standing: a novel by Deja King
For complete Library of Congress Copyright info visit;
www.joykingonline.com

A King Production
P.O. Box 912, Collierville, TN 38027

A King Production and the above portrayal log are trademarks of A King Production LLC

Dedication

This Book is Dedicated To My:

Family, Readers and Supporters. I LOVE you guys so much. Please believe that!!

Acknowledgements

Wow…I can't believe we've made it to Part 5! It's been a very long journey and I've LOVED every minute of it. To all my readers who have become die hard Precious Cummings aka Mills' fans I truly hope that I don't disappointment you with this installment and you believe I did 'our' girl justice!! Sit back, relax and enjoy the show!! Hugs and Kisses…

Your Literary Sweetheart,

Joy "Deja" King

Special Thanks To…

Linda Williams; We did it again, thanks for always being my biggest Cheerleader

Jonesy; You were the first radio personality that embraced my books! You set Bitch on fire in New York and I will forever love you for that!!

Tracy Taylor; Girl, have they figured out yet we will not stop!!

Ann Hopson; I see you girl..."You're so Pretty." ☺

Tazzy; I just adore you for being you!!

Keith Saunders; You're my dude!! Enough said...

Book Bullies; Watch out for them, they'll be taking over in 2010!!

Tureko "Virgo" Straughter, Renee Tolson, Jeanni Dixon, Ms KiKi, Andrea Denise, Sunshine716, Ms. (Nichelle) Mona Lisa, Lady Scorpio, Travis Williams, Brittney, Donell Adams, Myra Green, Leona Romich, Sexy Xanyell. To vendors and distributors like African World Books, Teddy Okafor, Black & Nobel, DaBook Joint, The Cartel, DCBookman, Tiah, Vanessa and Glenn Ledbetter, Junior Job, Anjekee Books, Andy Carter, Urban Xclusive DVD & Bookstore, Future Endeavors. Also, to Sherita Nunn, Troy Monaco, James Davis, Bev Johnson, Marcus & Wayne Moody, Trista Russell, Risque Café, Don Diva and Dolly Lopez...thank you all for your support!!

Special, special thanks to Cover 2 Cover Book Club; Christian Davis, Angela Slater, Pamela Rice, Ahmita Blanks, Melony Blanks, Marcia Harvey, Melinda Woodson, Tonnetta Smith, Tiffany Neal, Miisha Fleming, Tamika Rice and Bar. I so enjoyed our book chats for "Hooker to Housewife" and "Superstar". All of you ladies are wonderful!!

Last Bitch Standing

Precious

I've always been told that life's a bitch and then you die. If that's true, then I should've been dead a long time ago. But yet, here I was, still standing. And why? Because I was on a mission—driven by my need to demolish the one person who thought she was bad enough to outsmart me. I'll admit, the tables had been turned and it wasn't in my favor. But see, I had been left for dead on more than one occasion. My husband had died in my arms—or so I thought—and my daughter had been ripped out of my life. So this shit right here was nothing to me. Because like my man, Jay-Z says, "Difficult takes a day, impossible takes a week". Yeah, what I had to accomplish might take a little longer than that, but one thing was for sure: Maya was going the fuck down! I put that on everything.

"Are you ready to go?" Nico questioned, taking me out of the journey my mind was on of destroying Maya. It took me a few moments to answer, because I wasn't sure if I was ready to go. We had been doing time in Atlanta, based on a tip that led us nowhere so far. There was a so-called "Maya sighting" from one of the numerous private investigators we had hired to track the heffa down. I thought this one could actually be the real deal, but we'd hit yet another brick wall. Over the last few months every potential lead would come up empty. This chick had literally vanished, and took my husband and child with her. The shit had me perplexed an agitated like a motherfucker. I needed answers, but all I kept getting were more questions.

"I guess we're done here," I said, looking around my hotel room. I had been living out of my suitcase like a rapper on the road doing shows, and trying to make a come-up, and at the rate we were going, it wasn't going to stop anytime soon.

"Precious, don't get discouraged," Nico commented, as if reading my mind.

"I can't front, all this searching like we're in the dark with no flashlight is irritating the fuck outta me. I really thought this time, that scandalous trick was mine."

"And she will be...please believe that."

"I ain't got no choice, because if I didn't, I really wouldn't have a reason to live."

"You don't mean that."

"Yes the fuck I do! That deranged broad has my

child. I still love Supreme and I want my husband back, but hell, he's grown. He can protect himself. But Aaliyah, she can't, she needs me."

"I understand, and I promise there ain't a mountain I won't move to make that possible. I just don't want you to give up."

"Never that!"

As Nico drove to the airport, I looked out the passenger window, wondering if Maya really was out there somewhere in the ATL and we just simply missed her. Or worse, Maya had seen us and was now someplace gloating that she had once again won the game of hide and seek. I prayed that wasn't the case. It would be much easier for me to stomach that we had simply been directed to the wrong city, than to find out that Maya was still here, carrying on with a life she'd stolen from me.

"Nico, I can't put my finger on it, but something keeps tugging at me as if there is some sort of clue or answer that we are leaving behind."

"You mean here in Atlanta?"

"Yeah, I can't shake it."

"Precious, we've been here for weeks and come up with nothing."

"I know, but my gut keeps telling me something is here for us. I don't know what it is, but the feeling is so strong."

"So, what do you want to do, stay? I mean, supposedly

from what another investigator told us, there are some very good leads in Philadelphia. This tip seems reliable."

"And so did all the other ones, but we ain't got shit!"

"I know you're frustrated. So the fuck am I, but we can't stop looking!"

"I know that. Shit, I don't want to stop looking! I can fuckin' taste that bitch's blood like I'm a damn vampire. We ain't gon' never stop looking, but it's just this feeling I got. But it could be my agitation fuckin' with me."

"I think that's exactly what it is."

"Yeah," I sighed, falling back in my seat. "Let's take this flight to Philly. It could turn out to be beneficial… at least I hope so."

"Me too."

"Delta flight 1018 to Philadelphia will begin boarding in fifteen minutes," I heard the lady announce as Nico and I walked up.

The waiting area was jam packed, so clearly the flight was full. Although I had lived in New York for the majority of my life, I had never been to Philly even though it was damn near just down the street. I wouldn't know how to maneuver my way around even with a GPS, so luckily I had Nico with me. With hustling drugs for many years, Philadelphia had become like his own personal neighborhood playground, which was exactly what I needed.

"I'ma stop over there and get something to drink

4

before we get on the flight. Do you want anything?" Nico asked, as I was about to sit down.

"No, I'm straight."

"Cool. I'll be right back."

As Nico was walking towards his destination, I heard a female voice call out his name. I glanced over to see who the fuck was screaming for dude all the way in Atlanta. With Nico's baller status in the drug business, there was no question that he was nationally known in the street game. But hearing his name echoing through the airport threw me off for a second.

I watched intently as an extremely pretty chick greeted Nico with a too lengthy hug, as if he was her long lost love. I could damn near count every tooth in her mouth with how hard she was cheesing. But even with all that smiling and laughing the woman was doing, she had mad swagger. She definitely wasn't a sack chaser bum bitch who had nothing going on upstairs. She was a bitch that knew how to handle her business. That was clear from just observing her style game. The perfectly cropped jet black haircut, to the simple yet sexy sleeveless blouse, five pocket jeans with stud embroidery on the pockets, a leather belt with a prism shaped buckle and a large shoulder bag with what looked like hand braided chains and interlocking 'G' detail, topped off with some velvet high heel cuffed booties. Her entire outfit was jet black like her hair. The chick was on point and that was being peeped from one gangster to another.

As if Nico could feel me sizing their interaction up,

he pointed at me, then said something to the chick, and they started walking towards my direction. I played it cool as if I wasn't thinking about homegirl, and honestly, I wouldn't have been if it wasn't for the fact she seemed a little too comfortable for my taste around Nico. No doubt he wasn't my man any longer, but he was my first love, and a part of me would always be ready to snatch-a-bitch-up over him. I was territorial that way I suppose.

"Precious, I want to introduce you to a very good friend of mine," Nico said charmingly, as if giving me my respect. "This is CoCo Armstrong."

CoCo grinned at me and started to reach out her hand, but saw that mine were still folded in my lap, and quickly rescinded her gesture.

"Nice to meet you," I remarked coldly.

"Precious, I used to do a lot of business with CoCo before we lost touch," Nico said, trying to thaw the ice.

"Yeah, you mean before I had to sit down and take that vacation for a few months," CoCo countered, causing them to both chuckle.

I knew "vacation" was a code word for a bid in jail, which actually made me feel a little less icy towards the woman. I mean, don't nobody want to see the inside of a cell, but from one female to another, if you're able to do it and come out looking as good as she did, then I had to give her props off of that alone. Clearly she did the time, and didn't let the time do her.

"CoCo is actually on the same flight as us," Nico informed me.

"Oh, you from Philly?"

"No, I'm actually from Atlanta, but I live in Philly now." I nodded my head as I continued to feel the chick out.

"We have to hang out while you're visiting Philly," CoCo suggested, turning her attention back to Nico.

"This trip is more business than pleasure. I doubt we'll have time to hang out." CoCo stared at Nico suspiciously, and then tried to eye me on the sly but I caught that shit. She was trying to figure the situation out without coming right out and asking.

"I understand, but if shit changes, you have my numbers now. Give me a call. If we can't kick it on some fun shit while you're in Philly, definitely hit me up about business. I got a new partner now, and we making major moves."

"Cool…that's what's up. I'll be in touch for sure."

CoCo gave Nico a goodbye hug and then said, "It was nice meeting you, Precious," before walking off. But I couldn't help but feel this wouldn't be the last time my path crossed with CoCo Armstrong.

Maya

I stared out at the open water of the bay, with the unobstructed view to the dockage, as Supreme lounged on the yacht with Aaliyah. The calmness of the ocean had almost tricked my mind into believing there wasn't a storm brewing, that with each day, I was constantly fighting to divert.

The Georgian-style mansion that I had been living in with Supreme was nothing more than a high-priced, exquisite prison. From the flowing hardwood espresso floors, indoor waterfall, magnificent glass double staircases and soaring ceilings with arches and pillars, it was the sort of layout that MTV's *Cribs* was built on back in their heyday. But for me, it represented fear—fear that it would all be taken away from me if even one of my skeletons stepped out of the closet.

Not only was Devon out there lurking in the shadows waiting to seek revenge, but there was also Precious, my one-time mentor that I had meticulously plotted on to steal her life. My plan had seemed to come together so beautifully…until my brother replaced his brain with his dick. Then, Devon's nasty ass got greedy. And finally thinking I left Precious for dead, I now know she is very much alive.

I remember like it was yesterday, when Supreme got the phone call about the estate in Beverly Hills. Kitty, the airhead realtor I convinced Supreme to hire, had called his attorney in an uproar because she told him that some woman showed up claiming to be Supreme's wife and threw her out the house. I could see the glimmer in Supreme's eyes when he thought Precious had finally come back to him. But that glimmer instantly turned to hatred and rage when his attorney added that Kitty also said Precious showed up with some man, and from the description given, it sounded exactly like Nico. When his attorney asked him what he wanted to do, I'll never forget what Supreme said:

"Let her have the house, but do not tell her my whereabouts. As far as you know, I've vanished and don't want to be found." He calmly hung up the phone, but less than two seconds later, he trashed the place. If I hadn't seen it with my own eyes, I would've sworn up and down that a tornado had hit.

Hours later when Supreme had finally half-way calmed down, he admitted to me that he believed Precious had shown up to tell him it was over, that she was leaving him for Nico, and not only did she want a divorce, but she also wanted their daughter. I could see that Supreme was letting his paranoia get the best of him. "I won't let that happen," he stated firmly. "I can't make Precious leave Nico, but I will fuckin' make sure she never takes Aaliyah away from me."

With that idea cemented in Supreme's head, it actually helped my need to stay in hiding, because in a way, he was hiding too, but for totally different reasons. He felt he was protecting Aaliyah, but I was trying to protect my secrets. I knew all it took was one conversation between him and Precious and my cover would be completely blown. All my lies would explode in my face, and Supreme wouldn't want anything to do with me. And the one plan I was trying to orchestrate to salvage our relationship, if and when he found out, wasn't coming together. Why? Because I needed Supreme to be a willing participant, which I couldn't make happen.

Even with all the anger he had against Precious after that phone call from his attorney, Supreme refused to even touch me. It was as if believing Precious had truly moved on and chose Nico had castrated him. His sexual desires were zilch. The shit had me straight tripping, and also making it impossible for me to get pregnant. I figured if shit did hit the fan, Supreme would never hurt me or abandon me if I was carrying his child, but if I couldn't get no dick, then we couldn't make no baby.

So, here I was, in a sexless relationship with a man

who devoted all his time to his daughter as he secretly yearned for his wife. But some of that shit needed to change rather quickly—mainly the sexless part—because the clock was ticking. No matter how low-key we remained, knowing how relentless Precious was, she would eventually find us. The more I thought about it, the more I realized how limited my options were. It was either wait to be gotten, or go do the getting. Whichever way I chose to move, there were great risks, but I needed to make a decision soon, because time wasn't on my side.

"I'ma take Aaliyah for a ride. We'll be back," Supreme said on his way out the front door. I was so preoccupied in my scheming that I hadn't even noticed or heard them come inside.

"Wait a minute, I'll come with you."

"That's okay. I want to spend some alone time with Aaliyah."

"What do you mean? You were just alone with her for over an hour sitting on the yacht. I'm sure Aaliyah won't mind sharing you with me for a car ride."

"Fine…come on," he responded with no enthusiasm. But I didn't fuckin' care. I had to try and break down the walls that Supreme had built up, and I had a much better chance of doing it by spending *some* time with him than none at all. With each passing day, that shade was getting thicker and thicker with him. If I didn't make some serious progress soon, we would go from sharing the same bed with no sex, to sleeping in separate bedrooms altogether. If that happened, it would be a done deal and my time would officially be up.

As Supreme drove down the coastline seeming to be in deep thought, I stared back at Aaliyah, who was falling asleep. There was no denying that with each day, she resembled her mother more and more. There was also no disputing that as she was getting older and her personality was making more of a breakthrough, she had also inherited Precious' fire. Armed with her mother's looks and personality, and her father's money, I knew for a fact that once Aaliyah reached a certain age, she would be a force to be reckoned with. I wasn't sure I wanted to be around to witness that, unless of course I could deliver her that little brother.

"Supreme, we need to talk," I said, more determined than ever to bring my thoughts to fruition.

"What do we need to talk about?"

"Us."

"Us," he repeated, slightly laughing.

"That sounded funny to you?" I was unable to hide my annoyance. Supreme looked over at me, and then turned his head back around, looking straight ahead.

"Is this conversation you're trying to have with me really necessary?"

"I think so."

"I think not," he replied matter-of-factly.

"So what, you want to be roommates now, Supreme? Is that it?"

"Where are you going with this?"

"No, the question is where are *you* going? We go from leaving Beverly Hills to start fresh in Miami, to now you treating me like we're strangers."

"It was your idea to move to Miami."

"True, but you weren't exactly fighting me on the suggestion! As a matter of fact, you said you were ready to leave the bullshit behind and try and regain your sanity. You don't remember that?"

"Of course I remember, but shit changed," he mumbled.

"Shit like what?" I demanded to know, raising my voice.

"Keep your voice down! Aaliyah is sleep!" he demanded, in a loud whisper.

I wanted to yell out that I didn't give a flying fuck whether his golden child was sleep or not, this was about me, but restrained myself. "Listen, I don't want to argue with you. I care about you and I love Aaliyah. If you don't want us to have that type of relationship no more, then I'm cool with that. I'll stay in one of the guest bedrooms and help you with Aaliyah until you find a full time nanny."

"Where will you go?"

"Does it really matter? Isn't the point finally being able to get rid of me?"

"Maya, you know I care about what happens to you."

"I understand that, but you clearly have a lot of

unresolved issues to work out, and I think the only way you'll be able to do that is if I give you your space." I was rambling on, saying some shit I figured would be in a self-help book, knowing I didn't mean not one fucking word. There was no way I was exiting that palatial crib I was luxuriating in, no matter if I felt like a prisoner or not. This was all game, and at the moment I had no clue whether it was working in my favor or not. But fuck, desperate times call for desperate measures. You have to keep tossing shit out there until something sticks. And with the curve balls I was throwing, trust me, no matter how skilled Supreme was, he wouldn't be able to dodge them all.

Precious

During our flight to Philly, I basically slept the entire time. Getting rest had become an afterthought for me these last few months, and my body was now using any opportunity it could get to reenergize. And the sleep did do me some good, because instead going to the hotel, I was ready to handle business.

"How much longer until we get to the spot?" I asked Nico as he drove down what seemed to be back roads.

After our flight landed, he swooped up the rental car and we were off and running. Actually, we did have one interruption. Nico stopped and chatted with the chick, CoCo for a few, promising he would make time to see her, if only briefly before he left town. I could hear her swearing it was about business, like she needed to clarify that for my benefit.

"For the first stop, in a few more minutes."

"First stop?" I asked confused, since I only knew about one."

"Yeah, I gotta go get us some artillery. We can't be running up in places wit' no sort of backup. Baby girl, you of all people know how niggas be gettin' down in the streets. We can't take no chances."

"You know, I feel you on that. It's just that you didn't mention nothing, so I figured you didn't think we needed it. Are you skeptical about the dude we're supposed to meet with? I hope this tip is legitimate."

"Anytime a motherfucker is giving up info, I'm skeptical, so that's why we need to be prepared for anything. The shit is supposed to be legit, but it's hard to call it at this point. Supposedly this cat got information on Devon's whereabouts. And since he was the nigga working with Maya, I'm sure he's been in touch with her."

"No doubt, and I can't wait to take Devon's sheisty ass out. I gotta special bullet for him."

"Hold up! We need Devon to lead us to Maya, then we can talk about that bullet you got with his name on it."

"No worries, I'ma make sure we got no more use for him before I lullaby that ass."

"Stay right here, I'll be back in two seconds," Nico said, pulling up to some store. "I'ma run in real quick and get our shit. These my people around here, so you'll be straight. But if anything seems suspicious, blow the horn. There's always that one knucklehead that might try you,"

Nico grinned.

"I'm good."

As Nico ran up in the small corner store, I began thinking about the great pleasure I would take in shutting Devon the fuck down. When I first laid eyes on him, I knew he wasn't shit, but I slipped up and didn't follow my initial gut instincts. And what a costly mistake that was. The whole time he had partnered up with Maya to take me down. Every time I reflected back on what went down, I got more pissed with myself for not paying attention to key signs.

The biggest one was when Devon killed Vernika during my fight with her. He claimed he was trying to protect me, but in reality, he was protecting himself. She could have blown his cover, and he wasn't taking any chances. I remember how angry I was when she died, because it literally led to a dead end, but it was also what made me soften up to Devon because my dumb ass thought he had my back. Yeah, Devon definitely had to catch hell for tricking me up.

Just like Nico said, within a few seconds he was back. "A'ight, we good now, let's go," he said, closing the driver's door.

"Damn, they must've had that shit already bagged up for you."

"Pretty much. I hit 'em up at the airport, letting him know I was on the way. Here, this yours," he said, handing me my weapon of choice—a nine millimeter with a silencer already attached.

"Cool! I feel better already."

About ten minutes later, Nico pulled up to a brick building on an eerily quiet street. "We're here."

"Damn, ain't nobody out today," I commented.

"Mostly elderly people live on this block. They're probably all inside." I followed Nico as we walked up the stairs, and he rang the doorbell. After several seconds passed, he rang the doorbell again and knocked on the door.

"Is the dude expecting you?"

"So I thought."

"Have you spoken to him?"

"Nope, he ain't got no phone."

"Not even a cell? How old is this dude?"

"I don't know, but he was told we were coming. Oh, that might be him right there," Nico said, looking over my shoulder. I turned around and noticed a man getting out of a dollar cab. He gave the driver some money and started walking in our direction.

"What up? You must be Nico."

"Yeah, and you must be Curtis."

"Yep. I hope you ain't been waiting long. I got held up over at my job. I'm on parole, and I can't fuck around and miss work or they'll toss me back in jail. I'm sure you understand."

"No doubt."

"Cool. Well, let's go inside." The dude nodded his head at me as he brushed past me to open the door.

When we got inside, he led us down some stairs.

He lived in a basement apartment. The building brought back memories of the projects I grew up in while living in Brooklyn. No matter how huge the mansions or fly the whips I pushed and the diamonds I rocked, the Brooklyn projects ran through my blood.

"So, I understand you got some information about Devon," I said, as soon as we got inside of dude's apartment and the door closed behind us. I wanted to get straight to the point, tired of constantly coming up empty.

"Yeah... umm... I ain't got nothing but some water and beer. Would you all like some?"

"No, we good," Nico let it be known, because he saw me slit my eyes, ready to cut up. "So, you got information for us?"

"I do," Curtis replied casually while popping open his beer before sitting down on a dingy vomit-brown colored sofa.

"Cool, so spill," Nico countered.

"Well, Devon used to do some work for my cousin who was from New York, before he got a fancy job working for some big time nigga in Beverly Hills." I knew dude had to be talking about Supreme.

"Has he still been in contact with him?" Nico further pried. I could tell that like me, he was ready for the nigga to get to the point.

"That's the thing. For months he didn't hear a peep outta dude. He figured shit was going real good for Devon, and my cousin was happy for him. Not me though. I always thought that nigga was a snake. He seemed real sneaky. Then, he used to make smart ass comments that my cousin got all the smarts and I was the dummy of the family, shit like that. I could tell he thought he was better than me, so I figured he got around all those fake ass Hollywood people and forgot where fuck he came from—you know, his homies back in the 'hood."

"Right," Nico nodded as if in agreement.

"But then, one day a few months ago, out of the blue, here comes Devon, calling my cousin saying he had got jammed up and needed some financial help. Because, you know, my cousin be making that major paper out in the streets. I used to make a little money myself before I got locked up. I used to be the…"

"Listen, we ain't got time to reminisce with you. Tell us what the fuck you know so we can bounce!" I spit, agitated with the nigga already.

"You have to excuse her. We had a long flight and she's a little restless."

I was vexed that Nico was making excuses for me, but I also understood why. But I can spot a full of shit clown, and this nigga sitting on the couch was one, with his crusty mouth, unkempt clothes and the long overdue haircut that was crying his name.

"I feel you. So, like I was saying, I used to be the man. Making money, living good, with countless women checking for me. You get locked up, come home with no bread, shit changes real quick."

I didn't know how much longer I could stand to

listen to this broke man's sob story.

"But I'm sure your cousin is looking out for you," Nico said, playing into this nigga's foolishness.

"Look around this joint. Do it seem like he's looking out for me? Naw, he say that wit' me just gettin' out the joint and being on parole, I'm too hot to fuck wit'. He gives me a few bucks every once in a while, but he one of those niggas that's funny wit' his money. Always saying you got to earn your way in life. You know, like they can actually take it wit' 'em once they die."

"I feel you. Then the money I agreed to pay you should come in handy."

"Most definitely."

"Cool. I'm sure the dude that linked us up already told you that once you've fully cooperated and I make sure the information is legit, we good."

"Oh, it's legit. I promise you that."

"So, let's hear it."

"But… umm… the thing is, I think I'ma need a little bit more money than we originally agreed to."

"Here the fuck we go with this bullshit!" I huffed, knowing this clown was gon' be a problem.

"How much more money you talking about?" Nico asked him.

I wanted my hands on Devon more than anything, but I felt Nico was being way too soft with this clown. What if he was popping a bunch of lies? Maybe at one time his cousin knew where Devon was, but maybe he didn't know shit now, and dude was taking us for a ride.

"You tell me. For you to come all this way, the information must be pretty important to you."

"How about I double the money?"

"That number is sounding better," Curtis nodded, but from the expression on his face that still wasn't enough.

"How 'bout I triple it," Nico added.

"Fuck that!" I barked, jumping over the raggedy table in front of the couch Curtis was sitting on, while pulling out my heat at the same time. Before he had time to blink, my nine millimeter was pressed against his temple.

"Precious, calm the fuck down!" Nico yelled out.

"Nah, this nigga play too much! See, Nico is the patient one, I'm not. I will take you out this fuckin' world and not think nothin' of it." I really didn't want to blast this nigga just in case the information he had was on the up-and-up, but I couldn't let him know that. He had to believe that I would not think twice about laying his ass out unless he got to running his mouth.

"Man, you need to calm your girl down! She trippin!"

"I run this show! And if I say you gotta fuckin' go, then that's what it is!" I roared. The dude stared over at Nico with pleading eyes, but Nico just shrugged his shoulders and followed my program.

"You trippin, ma! I ain't mean no harm. I was gonna give you the information."

"Then stop running yo' mouth about bullshit and tell us what the fuck you know…now!"

Curtis swallowed hard before speaking. His body was trembling, so I knew he was shook and really believed I didn't give fuck about blowing his brains out.

"You gon' still give me the money though, right?" he finally said.

"Yeah, the fuckin' money you originally agreed to, you greedy motherfucker!" I said jamming the gun harder to his head.

"Devon is in Philly. He came back to do some work for my cousin. 'Cause like I told you, my cousin believes you got to earn your money. He ain't giving you shit."

"You got an address on him?" Nico asked.

"Yeah, it's written down on a piece of paper in my pocket."

"Stand up!" I ordered. "Which pocket?"

"The back one on the left hand side." I reached inside his pocket and pulled out the paper and handed it to Nico.

"Now can I get my money?"

"How do we know we can find him here?" Nico asked, looking up.

"I promise you it's good. But if I was you, I would catch him alone. My cousin surrounds himself with a lot of men that are paid to shoot first and ask questions later, Devon being one of them."

"Who is your cousin?"

"His name is Delondo, and right now he got most of Philly on lock. Just be careful, especially running around with this firecracker you got right here," he said, nudging his head in my direction.

"Nico, give this nigga his money so we can get the fuck outta here."

"Listen, if this shit turns out to be garbage, we will come back for you, and this time I'll let my girl have it her way," Nico stated before handing Curtis his dough.

"It's good, believe me."

"And don't go running your mouth letting anybody know what went down here," I added.

"Are you crazy? My cousin would have my ass! But I don't like Devon... never have, so I don't give a fuck what happens to him. His punk ass always thought he was better than me, but he had to come back begging my cousin for a job. That's what the nigga gets. He deserves whatever he got coming his way!"

I could have not agreed with that statement more. Devon was sitting almost right next to Maya on the loser totem pole.

"Devon here we come," I smiled, finally feeling we were making some real headway in our quest to find and destroy Maya.

Maya

Determined not to let Supreme call my bluff, I did exactly what I said I would—moved into one of the guest bedrooms. I really didn't have a choice. After our initial conversation in the car, I thought Supreme would make an effort to get closer to me, but he didn't change up shit. I was sleeping on one side of the bed, and him on the other. If I stayed, then he would believe I was just running off at the mouth and had no backbone to stick with what I threatened to do. So, a couple of days ago while he was out, I got my belongings together and moved to one of the bedrooms down the hall. When Supreme came home and realized what I did, even though he didn't say shit, I could tell he was surprised. I peeped him checking the closets to see if I had really taken everything, and motherfuckin' right, I did. I took it all, even down to the soap I liked to use.

He could act hardcore if he wanted to, but he would eventually miss me, if only because he no longer had a warm body next to him in bed. Hell, I missed him already, but this had to be done. *You gotta fuckin' do what you gotta do to get what you want.* I mean, isn't that what Precious would say? As much as I couldn't stand that bitch, I still found myself using her play book with every scam I tried to run, especially on a man—her man in particular.

As I started thinking about what my next move should be, the ringing of my cell phone distracted me. I looked to see who it was, and immediately recognized the number. "Hey, I've been waiting to hear from you. Any news?"

"Nothing on Precious, but I do have a lead on Devon."

"Where is he?"

"On the East Coast."

"Steve, can you be a little bit more specific?"

"I last tracked him in the Bronx, but I don't believe that's where he's residing. I think he was only visiting. By the time I found out where he was in the Bronx, he had already left, so I lost track of him."

"Yeah, he got family in the Bronx. He was probably visiting them. But fuck, he can be anywhere now!"

"I'm working on some leads. I've been asking some questions to the neighborhood people, but you know I don't want to scare them off because they think I'm the police or something."

"Whatever to that! With the money I'm paying you, I just want you to get an exact location on him, and let me know the minute you do."

"I will."

"And what's the hold up on Precious?"

"She must be staying on the move, because I can't get a lead on her for nothing."

Yeah, she's probably too busy looking for my ass to stay still, I thought to myself. "A'ight, just keep me posted," I said before ending the call.

I was putting the money I took from my brother after I killed him and burned the house down to good use. Once I was certain Precious was alive, I paid a pretty penny to have Steve track both Devon and Precious. I wanted to find them before they found me. The only downside was that Steve wasn't an assassin that I would have to handle personally. Although someone who could execute both was ideal, I didn't want to take a chance and get swindled by an undercover cop and end up in jail behind a murder plot. At this point in the game, I had to be very careful with every move I made, or all eyes would be on me.

Knock…knock…knock

"Come in."

"Hey, I have to run out for a couple of hours. Aaliyah is sleep, but can you watch her in case she wakes up?"

"No problem." *Now this motherfucker wants me to be his personal babysitter with no benefits! This some straight bullshit!*
"I appreciate that."
"I know you do. So go 'head, take your time, do what you need to do. I'll be here when Aaliyah wakes up," I smiled, trying to sound sincere. This was all about who could outwait who without snapping. But those who are patient usually win it all, and that's what I was counting on when it came to Supreme. He figured that since I wasn't getting no dick and moved to the guest bedroom, I would turn on him and not want to watch his prized daughter anymore. But no, I planned on doing the exact opposite. I mean, being a nurturing mother figure to Aaliyah after I had Precious chained up in a basement, was how I suckered Supreme in the first place. Shit, I was willing to take it back to the basics and start over again.

"Thanks, Maya," Supreme said, sounding surprised by my gracious behavior. Clearly my act worked. He left my bedroom, and I went over to the window and watched him make a call before he got into his car.

"I wonder who Supreme is calling. It's probably nothing," I thought out loud, but the curiosity was heavy on my mind.

I left my bedroom and decided to take advantage of being alone with only a sleeping baby to worry about. I went downstairs to Supreme's office, and of course it was locked. But unbeknownst to him, one afternoon while he was taking a long nap, I took the key and had a duplicate made. I even let Aaliyah tag along on my adventure to make sure she didn't disturb her daddy and wake him up before I finished doing what I needed to get done.

This would only be my second opportunity to use it, as I was hardly ever in the house alone. Supreme rarely went anywhere, and if he did, it was never long enough where I would feel comfortable doing some serious snooping.

When I opened the door, I headed straight for his mahogany desk. There were a lot of folders and a ton of paperwork, but it was mostly business contracts, legal correspondence—nothing I gave a fuck about. I continued to go through his drawers, being very careful to leave everything in place. Luckily, Supreme wasn't one of those anal types that had all his shit in perfect order.

Finally, something caught my eye, the reason being because it was bank documentation, but it wasn't in Supreme's name. It was some company called Direct Express Enterprises. There were a ton of large deposits being made, but the bizarre part was that they were all going to the same account, to a person by the name of Arnez Douglass. It was as if a dummy account was set up just to transfer money to this one individual. *Hmmm, who in the world is Arnez Douglass, and why is Supreme giving him all this fuckin' money?* I wrote the dude's name down and the address associated with his account on a post-it, because he was clearly somebody of importance if Supreme was hitting him off with this sort of cash. I checked around one last time to make sure everything was in place before leaving. After locking the door, I went back upstairs to my bedroom to make a call.

"Hey, Steve."

"You can't possibly think I have some new information for you already. I just got off the phone with you less than an hour ago."

"No, of course not. I need you to do something else for me."

"Is it pertaining to the case I'm already on?"

"No, it's something different."

"Different case, different money."

"Have you had any problems getting paid from me so far?"

"No, and I want to keep it that way."

"You worry about doing what I've hired you to do, and let me worry about the money. Are we clear?"

"We're clear. So, what do you need?"

"You have a pen?"

"Yep."

"Okay, write this name and address down," I said, speaking slowly and clearly so he wrote the shit down accurately.

"So, who is Arnez Douglass?'"

"That's what I'm going to pay you to find out."

"So, you know nothing about him?"

"Nope. How long is it going to take you?"

"Not sure, but give me at least a couple of days."

"I can do that. I'll be waiting."

When I got off the phone, I laid back on the bed and stared up at the soaring ceiling. I was now consumed with knowing everything I could about this Arnez guy. I had a feeling that whoever he was, Supreme would've preferred it if he remained a secret. But secrets are never safe with me, and I was determined to get to the bottom of it.

Precious

We had been by the spot Curtis gave us for a few days straight, and there was no sign of Devon. After the second day, I was ready to go back to Curtis' crib and stomp his ass, but Nico convinced me to make sure we had been conned before lashing out. So, by us staking out the location each day all day, we pretty much knew the routine of mail delivery.

On the fourth day, since we knew the mail person was a middle-aged woman, we decided to use Nico as bait. I hid in the car while he pretended to be going into the building where Devon supposedly lived. He turned on his charm and flirted with the mail lady. She ate that shit up. Nico convinced her that he was a family member who was now staying at the apartment, and he would be more than happy to take the mail. From what I could see, he didn't have to do too much convincing. She practically stuffed the mail down his shirt, along with her phone number. And to my surprise, Curtis had told the truth, because the mail was addressed to Devon. We figured Devon was out of town, either for business or personal, and we would have to wait it out.

"Yo, I was considering doing something, but I wanted to see how you felt about it first," Nico said, as we sat in the rental car across the street, watching Devon's crib.

"Ask me."

"I wanted to call CoCo and see if she knew any information on this Delondo cat, since Devon work for him. I mean, if he's supposed to be a major nigga in the drug game for Philly, and she's in the same business, maybe she can be helpful."

"Like instead of us sitting here every damn day twiddling our thumbs waiting for the fuck to show up, she may actually be able to tell us an exact day…helpful like that?"

"I don't know if she could tell us the day, but something. Maybe Devon got another spot he rests at that Curtis don't know nothing about. But what I do know is this Philly drug game is very cliquish, and everybody be watching how each clique moves."

"But you know mad people here. Ain't nobody else you can call besides CoCo that might have some useful info?"

"Yeah, I do know a lot of people here, but with CoCo I can trust she won't run off at the mouth, making announcements that I'm inquiring about homeboy."

"So, you trust her?"

"Are you jealous? Because you don't have any reason to be."

"Don't flatter yourself. I just want to have as few people in our shit as possible. But if you trust her, then make the call." And that's what he did. I could hear her through the phone, acting all extra excited to hear from Nico. I had to admit that it *was* jealousy making me catch an attitude, because the chick hadn't did shit to me, and I couldn't stand her ass.

"That was a quick conversation. I guess she didn't know shit."

"It's not that. She wants us to talk in person. With her getting caught up in that fed shit and being locked up, she don't like to discuss nobody who is affiliated with the drug game on the phone."

"That's understandable. So, are we about to meet up with her now?"

"No, she's in the middle of some business at the moment. She said tonight would be better for her. But I know you're probably tired and could use the rest, so you don't have to come with me. I can handle it on my own."

"I'm good. We can go together. This a team effort, remember?"

"Of course, and you know I always enjoy your company. So, do you want to head back to the hotel, rest a little bit before we head out tonight?"

"That works for me."

When we got back to the hotel, I went in my room and took a long hot shower. I needed the time alone to try and clear my mind, if only for a few minutes. But instead of thinking about absolutely nothing, I wondered what Aaliyah was doing at the very moment, and if Supreme was holding her. I missed the two of them to the point that pain had almost become numb. It was as if my heart had built a shield around it, because if I actually continued to feel how much it ached, I would die from heartbreak.

What made it worse was that I knew Supreme had fucked Maya. I remember vividly how she rubbed it in my face. Devon held my body firmly while Maya beat the shit outta me with those brass knuckles, and taunted me about her getting dicked down by my husband. I could tell by the look in her eyes and the venom in her voice that it was true. I also knew that she didn't have his heart—which belonged to me and always would. But it didn't make it any easier to accept. But Supreme and I had been through so much, and this was another hurdle we would overcome together…or so I hoped.

But I wasn't naïve to the fact that a lot of damage had been done on both parts. He knew about my indiscretion with Nico, and with all the poison Maya had drenched on him, Supreme was probably convinced I was somewhere laid up with Nico right now, getting my fuck on. It would take all my strength and his to salvage our marriage, and with the more time that passed with us apart, the more worried I was becoming.

When I stepped out of the shower, the hot water hadn't washed away any of the burdens placed upon me. If anything, it made them worse. I stared at my reflection in the mirror and thought back to being held captive in that house, and the first time Mike let me take a shower. When I first saw my face again after all that time, it almost startled me. I barely recognized myself. Here I was again, feeling the same way, but this time for a different reason. No longer were my cheeks sunken, or dark circles around my eyes, or my complexion dull from being deprived of sunlight. In fact, many would say I was glowing and looked radiant due to my deep tan, courtesy of the hot summer weather. But I knew better. The fire in my eyes was slowly simmering out, and it was because everything I loved seemed to be slipping further out of my grasp.

Ring…ring…ring

"Hello."

"How long will it take you to get ready?"

"I thought you said we weren't meeting up with homegirl for at least a couple of hours."

"CoCo just called and said she wrapped up shit sooner than she anticipated and we could meet now."

"Give me thirty minutes," I said, ending the call. I wondered if CoCo was rushing Nico, thinking he was coming solo, or if she knew I would also be in attendance. Just in case she didn't, I decided to put on the only one cute dress I brought with me. All my other clothes were street gear, since none of my recent trips had been for pleasure. But I figured for emergency purposes, a woman should always come prepared with at least one sexy item, and this one was mine.

Exactly thirty minutes later, Nico came knocking on my door, and lucky for him, I was dressed and ready to go.

"Wow, you look incredible," were the first words out of his mouth when I opened the door. "For the last couple of months all I've seen you in is sweats and sneakers. I almost forgot how hot you are."

"Funny!"

"I'm joking. You know I love your casual around-the-way-girl look. But this is nice too. I hope you dressed up for my benefit."

"Let's go. We don't want to keep your friend, CoCo waiting."

When we pulled up to a restaurant in Center City, I was actually hungry, which was surprising to me since my appetite had been pretty much void lately. "This spot is cute, like they may have some good food in here."

"You're hungry?" I could understand why Nico sounded astounded.

"Yep! And trust me, you can't be more surprised than I am. So instead of dwelling on it, I'ma try to enjoy a fuckin' great ass meal. Hopefully they have a big juicy steak."

"Damn, you really are hungry. Good for you!" Nico laughed, playfully nudging me on our way into the restaurant.

When we got inside, there was a hostess greeting us with huge smile. "Welcome. Are there only two in your party?"

"Actually…"

"Nico, over here!" CoCo stood up, waving her hand before he finished his sentence, but now there was no need to. The hostess trailed behind us with two menus, and put them down on the table once we sat down.

After hugging up on Nico, CoCo turned her attention to me. "Precious, what a cute dress you're wearing."

"Thank you," I said, dryly.

"Nico, I'm glad you were able to meet up with me. I know this is supposed to be strictly about what's going on with you, but I couldn't help but try and take advantage of this time and discuss a little business."

"I wouldn't expect anything less from you, CoCo. If you didn't do that, I would say you were slipping."

"And you know that ain't happening. I'm always about my business. Speaking of business, here comes my partner now."

My back was towards the door so I couldn't see who her partner was, and honestly, I didn't fucking give a shit.

Nico might've not cared that she managed to turn this dinner into her own personal business meeting, but I wanted to reach across the table and slap the chick so hard it would knock out the two carat clear rocks adorning her ears.

"Nico, Precious, this is Genesis, my business partner."

The very first thought that popped into my head when my eyes landed on Genesis was God had truly been good to that man. He was unbelievably gorgeous. And trust me, I knew gorgeous men, because both Nico and Supreme were running strong in the race for the looks department. But the dude standing before me had something special that I had never witnessed in another man. I don't know if it was called swagger, the X-factor… but whatever it was, Genesis was winning the race with it hands down.

"It's a pleasure to meet you both. CoCo has spoken very highly of you, Nico," Genesis continued, as he shook Nico's hand. "I hope we'll be able to do business together."

"Same here."

"I apologize for running late, but I had to put my son to sleep. He's so stubborn," Genesis said, affectionately.

"No problem, we just got here ourselves," Nico let him know.

"How is my baby?" CoCo smiled, gazing lovingly into Genesis' eyes.

"You all have a child together?" That shit slipped

out so quickly that I hoped it didn't come off as if I sounded surprised.

"No, but I always refer to Amir as my baby."

"Truth is, you have become like a mother to him since the day he was born," Genesis stated as he gently touched CoCo's hand.

There were so many questions running through my head, mainly like; where was the child's birth mother? Because there was no way in the world any sane woman would leave a man like him. But that was none of my motherfuckin' business, so I opted to keep my mouth shut.

"Thank you. You know I love him like he was my own." I was trying to get a read on their relationship but it was tricky. I couldn't tell if they were fucking or if the closest CoCo had gotten was only making love to Genesis in her mind.

"That's a beautiful thing, CoCo. It's nice hearing about this motherly side of you. Normally with you, it's straight business, but I see you got a sensitive side for the babies," Nico teased.

"Enough of this. Let's get back to business," CoCo slightly giggled. "So, before we discuss the proposal we have about our shit, let's discuss what you need to know."

"Ms. Armstrong, will you be having your customary bottle of champagne for the table?" the waiter asked, interrupting my curiosity of needing to know if CoCo and Genesis relationship was platonic or not.

"Yes, unless the two of you would like something

else instead."

"Champagne is fine with me. How about you, Precious?"

"It's fine with me too."

"Wonderful. I'll be back shortly with your champagne and to take your orders."

"Thank you, Roberto."

"My pleasure, Ms. Armstrong."

"Now, back to you," CoCo said, directing her attention back to Nico. "You wanted to get some information on Delondo."

"I really needed some information on someone who works for Delondo. His name is Devon."

"I can easily find out that information for you. Delondo is a major player out here. One of his lieutenants is actually very cool with one of our top workers. We're considering merging on some business together, but details haven't been worked out."

"Well, I'ma be straight up with you. I have no beef with the dude Delondo, but the nigga, Devon is a problem that needs to be taken care of. I'm letting you know in case that will jeopardize whatever you're trying to make happen over there."

"No, I can't see that being a problem. The nigga, Devon can't be an important member of his team, because I haven't heard of him. Have you, Genesis?"

"No, I haven't."

"If you don't mind me asking, why is finding this Devon person so important?" CoCo inquired.

"Because we're looking for a young lady named Maya Owens, and Devon might be able to help us locate her."

"Maya Owens," Genesis said, with a hint of interest in his voice.

"Yes, do you know her?" I directed my question right at Genesis, locking eyes with him.

"No, I don't."

Without skipping a beat, Nico continued on, and CoCo was giving him her full attention, but Genesis, not so much. He had now become lost in his own thoughts, and I knew it was because he was lying. He did know a Maya, and I had a strong feeling it was the same Maya we were looking for.

"Excuse me for one second, I have to make a phone call," I heard Genesis whisper to CoCo before excusing himself from the table. The two of them were so enthralled in their conversation that when I told Nico that I had to use the restroom, he smiled at me, nodded his head, and kept talking.

I couldn't get out my seat fast enough. I made a direct beeline to Genesis, who was in the corner of the hallway trying to have a discreet conversation. His back was facing away from me, so I tried to sneak and see if I could hear anything he was saying, but dude was talking too low. He kept the call short, and when he was done, I made my move.

"Genesis, how do you know Maya?" I kept my tone even and firm.

"I told you, I don't know a Maya. Now, if you'll excuse me…"

I shifted my body, positioning it so that I almost had him boxed in. "I know you don't give a damn about me."

"I don't even know you."

"Exactly. That's why I know you don't give a damn… and it's cool. But what's not cool is if you don't tell me what you know about Maya. Her treacherous ass is with my husband and my daughter, and I need to find them before it's too late."

"I don't understand."

"What the fuck don't you understand? Your little son that you were just gushing over a few minutes ago, well that's how the fuck I feel about my own daughter! And Maya has schemed to the lowest level to keep me away from her and Supreme. Now, if you have some information that can get me back to my family, then you need to tell me."

"So you're Supreme's wife."

"That's right, I am."

"Precious Cummings—excuse me—I mean Precious Mills. It's nice to finally place the name with the face."

Maya

As I lounged by the pool in my taupe suede string bikini, which was clearly made to prance around in and not for swimming purposes, I wondered how long it would take to catch Supreme's attention. I had lathered my body in baby oil so my skin was glistening. At first, I was even going to put on some open-toe stilettos, but felt that would make this entire setup too obvious. But trying to seduce him in this scorching heat was starting to get the best of me. But I had no other way to pull this shit off. I couldn't walk around the house butt-ass-naked. That would surely send the "desperate" bells ringing. Lounging by the pool on a hot summer afternoon was very conceivable, even if I didn't know how to swim.

As the time kept ticking away, Supreme was nowhere

to be seen. Luckily I had brought out plenty bottles of water to make this situation not so unbearable. But the more the heat beat down on me, the rawer my nerves became. *Where the fuck is this nigga at? I know he took Aaliyah out for breakfast, but that was hours ago. He play too much. Don't he know I got a seduction going on today?*

As I became more and more frustrated, I got jarred out my thoughts by the sound of my cell phone ringing.

"Hello," I answered without even checking to see who was calling. I knew that only a handful of people had my new number after getting rid of the old one, which of course was done mainly to dodge Devon's ass.

"I have good news and great news. Which one would you like first?"

"Good news."

"The good news is that I found out some interesting information about Arnez Douglass. Not to get into your personal business, but if he's someone you're interested in dating, stay the hell away from him."

"Why?"

"He's a drug lord and a dangerous one at that; although I've never heard of a harmless drug lord."

My P.I. was borderline corny. So I gave him a pass. He didn't understand that words like 'drug lord' and 'dangerous' equaled intriguing to a bitch like me. "Continue."

"His operations used to be based in Atlanta, but for the past year he's been operating out of Philadelphia, which leads me to the great news."

"I'm waiting."

"That is where Devon is now living…in Philadelphia."

"Really?"

"Yes *and*," he stressed. "I have an address on him."

"Steve, I'm very pleased with you today," I admitted in almost a singing tone.

"I knew you would be. It might take me some time, but I'm very thorough and I always come through."

"Yes, you do."

"So what's my next move?"

"You stay there and keep an eye on Devon until I'm able to come."

"So, you're coming to Philadelphia?"

"Exactly. I'm on the first flight out tomorrow. I'll let you know where to meet me so I can get the address from you and pay you your money."

"Sounds like a worthwhile trip to me."

"I figured you'd say that. I'll be in touch." Right when I was about to rejoice on the good news from Steve, Supreme finally decided to bring his ass home.

"I see you're doing some sunbathing."

"Yep, you know they say the sun energizes you."

"Oh, I thought it just made you sweat." I sensed some sarcasm in his voice, but chose to ignore it.

"So, where's Aaliyah? I missed her today," I lied, but it sounded good.

"Sleep. After we went to eat, I took her to the park and she's exhausted."

"I'm sure she loved spending time with her daddy.

She always does."

"Yeah, being with her makes everything feel right."

For a brief moment, I almost felt guilty for being so jealous of Supreme's relationship with his daughter. It was obvious the nigga truly adored her, but instead of feeling happy for him, it made me disgusted. I mean damn, why couldn't I have grown up with a daddy that gave a fuck about me? Shit, growing up, my daddy wasn't even around. I had to count on Mike to fill them shoes, and he did a poor motherfucking job at it. He was too busy hustling in the streets to give a damn about me. All he would toss my way is some cash. *Life is so fuckin' unfair,* I thought.

"I'm sure children do that for you. Hopefully, one day I'll have some of my own and I can experience it for myself."

"It'll happen for you."

Yeah, motherfucker, if you would just get with the program and give me some dick! You're the hold up with the process, not me!

"I think so too, but not right now. I have so much more I need to accomplish." I threw that at the nigga to put him at ease. If I told him I was looking to become "sperminated" immediately, he probably wouldn't even breathe in my direction again.

"That's a good idea. You're young, and you should experience a lot more before settling down with a child."

"My sentiments exactly." I smiled and turned over on my stomach so my plump ass was smacking dude in his face.

"So, what's up with you tonight?"

I could see Supreme trying his damnedest to look in every direction but the flesh of my oil downed glistening butt. "Packing."

"You're going on a trip." He raised one of his eyebrows. I wasn't sure if it was out of surprise, or from disappointment.

"I wouldn't call it a trip. My mom called me. She didn't sound too good. I think maybe she's lonely, so I told her I would come visit."

"How long are you gonna be gone?"

"A few days, unless you want me to stay longer?"

"No, I was just curious. I think it's good you're going to spend some time with your mother. I know your relationship with her has never been good. It's never too late to change that."

"True. I guess this trip will let me see if that's possible."

"So, when are you leaving?"

"Tomorrow morning."

"That soon?"

"If I didn't know better, I would think you were going to miss me." I was a tad flirty with my delivery to give Supreme and easy opening to reciprocate if he so desired.

"It's nice having you around...I mean, you really help me out a lot with Aaliyah."

Oh, so now this motherfucker mad because his live in babysitter is going out of town. Listen to this bullshit right here! Niggas!

"I'ma miss her. Aaliyah is a wonderful little girl. I'll

have to keep my trip brief if only because I'll miss her so much." Right when Supreme was parting his lips to respond, I glided my body in an awkward way so one of my nipples slipped out my bikini top. "Is something wrong?" I asked innocently, pretending I hadn't even noticed I was giving Supreme a mouthful view of by right tit.

"No, I'm good. I have business to attend, so I'ma leave you to your sunbathing."

"Okay, I'll talk to you later on." *That's right, baby, hurry away so you don't give into temptation and tap this ass. But run all you want. Eventually I'll catch you out there slipping, and when that happens, you'll at least have to put up with me for a minimum of eighteen years.* The very idea of that put the biggest smile on my face.

When I arrived in Philadelphia, I had two missions: kill Devon, and meet Arnez Douglass. I wanted to know why Supreme was filtering all that cash to a drug dealer. *Were they in business together? If so, was it drug related? And why would Supreme feel the need to do that, because he's making a shit load of money in the music industry...or at least I assumed but then again with some people they can never make enough paper*, I thought to myself as I tried to figure all the shit out.

I was becoming impatient waiting for Steve at some raggedy ass diner. I was ready to find Devon, kill him, and then spend the rest of my trip finding out what the connection was between Supreme and Arnez.

"Can I get you anything else?" the waitress asked, smacking way too hard on her gum.

I really wanted to say, 'Just you staying the fuck out my face,' but instead I said, "Another Coke." I didn't need to bring any unnecessary attention to myself, and cussing out the waitress would do exactly that. A few seconds later, Steve walked in, and I was damn happy to see him because I was ready to go.

"Sorry I'm late, but I got lost looking for this place," he explained as soon as he sat down.

"That's why I picked it because it's hard to find."

"I get it."

"I figured you would, since trying to locate people is supposed to be your specialty."

"And it is," he said, sliding a piece a paper across the table.

"I take it this is the address I need."

"Indeed."

"Did you also dig a little deeper on that other information I asked you for?"

"I don't know why you're interested in this man. I told you he is a ruthless criminal. If anything, you should be trying to stay away, not get closer. I don't understand the logic behind that."

"That's not your concern. I have my reasons. Now, what did you find out?"

"From my understanding, when he's in town he dines

every day at a restaurant called Lacroix at the Rittenhouse Hotel. So much so, that he even has a certain table he always sits at."

"Interesting. What else?"

"He has a condo at the Murano in Center City."

"Is he in town now?"

"As of yesterday he was, because he had lunch at the Lacroix."

"And you know this because?"

"I paid one of the waiters that works there a nice piece of change that you're going to reimburse me for, to inform me when he came."

"He could've been lying."

"No, because once he called, I went to the location to confirm."

"What sort of confirmation?"

"See for yourself." Steve handed me a 9x12 envelope.

"So, this is what Arnez Douglass looks like. Not bad...not bad at all," I said, staring at the photos of him leaving the restaurant. "Who is that man with him?"

"His bodyguard. The waiter said he never leaves his side. From what I understand, a few months ago his other bodyguard was killed."

"Do you know what happened?"

"The car blew up, actually near this restaurant. The food must be awfully good for him to still go back," Steve remarked sarcastically.

"This is getting more interesting by the minute. So, I'm assuming this is the best place to run into Mr.

Douglass?"

"After what I just told you, you still want to make contact with this man?"

"I'm sorry, maybe I need to check my birth certificate, but I don't remember you being my father. So, moving on, answer my question."

"The waiter said he's supposed to be there tomorrow for lunch at noon. I told him to call me the moment he arrives."

"Perfect! So then you call and give me the heads up. Now, what about Precious?"

"No luck," he confessed, shrugging his shoulders. Why is it so important for you to find Devon and Precious?"

"Do you always ask your clients this many questions?"

"Only the ones that pique my interest."

"And why do I interest you so much?"

"For one, you have to be the youngest client I've ever had, and I don't even understand how you can afford me."

I'm so happy I gave this nosey motherfucker a bunch of fake information, because he would probably investigate me too, if he hasn't already. He can try to pull up some shit on that fake name I gave him if he wants to, but he'll come up empty.

"So, are you going to answer my question or not?"

"You mean about why I'm looking for those two people?" Steve nodded his head. "They were very close friends of my brother, but somehow they lost touch. Before he died, he asked me to find them because he left them both something that was very meaningful to him."

"I see."

"The least I can do is fulfill his dying request. Especially since it's his money that's paying for it."

"What do you mean?"

"Our parents died years ago, and he had no other family, so I was the sole beneficiary of his insurance policy."

"I think it's admirable that you're carrying out your brother's wishes, but with whatever money you have left, I hope you're being careful and not letting it go to waste."

"I promise you, I'm putting his money to very good use. He would be proud."

Precious

"I don't give a damn what that motherfucker says, Genesis has some information on Maya!"

"Precious, ever since we left that restaurant the other night, you've been saying this same shit. And my questions to you are the same; how would Genesis know Maya? And if he did, why would he try to hide it?"

"If I knew the answers to those questions, we wouldn't be having this conversation right now!" I barked, sick of Nico not siding with me on this.

"Why is it so hard for you to believe that I'm right, and this nigga, Genesis is full of shit?"

"Because I don't get that impression of dude. He seems legit, like he's cool people."

"Cool people my ass! Don't let all that swagger fool

you, he's hiding some shit."

"So, you think he got swagger?" Nico glanced over at me and asked as he turned the corner headed towards Devon's crib. He got word from CoCo that Devon was due back in town any day now, so we decided to do some drive-bys until his ass popped up.

"I'm not even going there with you," I said, slitting my eyes.

"Going where? You made the comment."

"It ain't even worth expanding on. All I know is the nigga is lying, and I want to know why."

"Well, baby girl, if he is lying, which I personally don't believe, we have no way of finding out the truth. We have to keep our money on Devon knowing where Maya is."

"That's another thing."

"What?"

"Don't you think it's strange that Devon is in Philly working for this nigga, Delondo?"

"Maybe he and Maya thought they should keep some distance between them until shit cooled down. I mean, they killed Mike, and I know by now they know you didn't die in that fire. They're probably nervous. I know if it was me, that's what I would do."

"True."

As we sat across the street from Devon's apartment, I thought about all the players in this game. And I didn't give a fuck what Nico said, in my book, Genesis was now officially one of them. But what drove me crazy about him was that I couldn't figure out how he fit in. I wondered if he had been cool with Mike, but I never heard him mentioned, and Genesis wasn't a name you would forget. The not knowing was making my brain itch.

"I hope you ain't still thinking about that Genesis shit," Nico commented, knowing me all too well.

"No, I'm not."

"Stop lying. Precious. This is Nico you're talking to."

"I know who the fuck you are."

"Then admit I'm right...come on now."

"I'm not admitting shit, and stop harassing me and answer your phone," I said, punching his arm.

"I ain't done wit' you," he huffed before taking the call.

While Nico was on the phone, I continued playfully punching his arm and making faces, until I realized the shift in his tone. It suddenly turned serious. "What's wrong?" I immediately asked when he got off.

"That was Ricky."

"Is he okay?"

"He's fine. It's Ms. Duncan...she died a few days ago."

"What! What happened?"

"She had cancer."

"I didn't even know she was sick."

"Neither did her brother. He said supposedly she got diagnosed about a month ago, and by the time she found out, it had already spread."

"I can't believe Ms. Duncan is dead."

"Ricky tried to call you, but of course the number he had ain't good no more. That's why he called me, so I could let you know. They're going to put her to rest this Friday."

"I wanna go to her funeral. That woman did so much for me. I have to pay my respects and tell her goodbye."

"Say no more. We'll go. By the time we get back, Devon will fo' sure be in Philly, and we'll handle him then."

As I stood at the same cemetery where my mother was buried, watching Ms. Duncan's coffin being lowered into the ground, I couldn't help but think of how unfair life could be. Ms. Duncan was one of the kindest people I had ever met, yet she was dead, and a lowdown trick like Maya was running around, free as a bird, wrecking peoples' lives. There was no rationale in that.

"Precious, I'm so glad you came," Ricky said, giving me a hug.

"Of course I came. You know how much your sister meant to me."

"And you meant a great deal to her too. She loved you, and she was so proud of you."

"I don't know why. I haven't lived my life in the most Godly way."

"Let he who is without sin cast the first stone. And

that's nobody. My sister knew and understood that, and lived her life accordingly. I'll tell you again. She was so proud of you, Precious."

"Thank you, Ricky."

"You have nothing to thank me for. But I would like for you to do something for me."

"What is it?"

"Before you leave New York, stop by her house. She left something for you."

"Okay, I will."

"Good."

"Did you see where Nico went?"

"Yes, he's right over there," Ricky said, pointing towards a tree behind me a few feet away.

"Thanks, but I'll definitely see you before we leave," I said, giving Ricky a hug goodbye.

Being at the cemetery where both my mother and Ms. Duncan were buried flooded me with sadness. I wanted to leave and escape the pain, because all I kept thinking about was Aaliyah and her losing me like I had lost the two most important women in my life.

"Nico, I'm ready to go." I could see he was in the middle of a conversation with someone, but I didn't care.

"Can you give me a few minutes?"

"No, I want to leave now."

"Babe, I know this is hard for you. Just give me a couple minutes." Nico lifted up my chin gently, and it was hard to deny his request. In his eyes, I could see he felt my pain.

"You must've been very close to her," I heard the man say who had been talking to Nico. His back was facing me when I walked up, so I hadn't paid him any attention... until now.

"Excuse me?" The attitude and annoyance was obvious in my voice because I didn't try to hide it. For the life of me, I couldn't understand why this nobody was inviting himself into my personal space. Just because he had been speaking with Nico didn't give him the right to talk to me.

"There's no need to get upset," Nico said, placing his hands on my shoulders as if to massage my frustrations away and diffuse the hostility.

"It's understandable you would be upset. She was a wonderful woman," the man continued, trying to force me into some dialogue. I turned to face the man for the first time, that's when he extended his hand and said, "I apologize. I should introduce myself. I'm Quentin Jacobs."

I shook his hand, and I instantly remembered meeting him at the house where Mike had held me hostage, and I couldn't help but wonder if he remembered me too.

"Growing up, we all looked up to Quentin, and we still do," Nico grinned. "That was rude of me. I should've introduced you. Quentin, this is Precious Mills."

I quickly freed my hand from the man's grasp, but he wasn't deterred. "Precious, how did you know Ms. Duncan?"

"She used to take care of me when I was a little

girl."

"Really, I knew all the little girls Ms. Duncan used to take care of, and I don't remember a Precious Mills."

"What about Precious Cummings? That was her name before she got married," Nico informed Quentin, clearly in awe of him.

"No, that name doesn't sound familiar either."

"Then I guess you didn't know all the kids Ms. Duncan took care of after all. Now if you'll excuse me... Nico, I'll be waiting for you in the car."

For some reason, I had a strong urge to rush off and get away from that man from the very first time I met him. And even now he had this way of getting under my skin. I didn't know if it was due to the arrogance he exuded, or because it disgusted me how Mike, who had been at the top of his game at one time before he died, and Nico, who many considered to be a legend in the streets, was dick riding this nigga so hard. Whatever it was, I didn't want any parts of it.

"Did you have to be so cold to him?" Nico questioned when he got in the car.

"Cold to who?" I asked, pretending not to have a clue as to what he was talking about.

"Stop with the games, Precious. Why did you have to be so disrespectful to Quentin? That cat is a straight up Godfather in this game. The respect he garners extends from the East to West Coast, trust me on that."

"I don't give a damn. Remember I told you that he came to visit Mike when I was being held hostage?"

Nico was quiet for a minute, as if thinking back to the conversation. "I do remember you mentioning something about that."

"Yeah, he didn't even acknowledge that shit."

"That was months ago, and it was only briefly. He probably doesn't remember that shit."

"You mean the same way Genesis doesn't know who Maya is."

"There you go on that Genesis shit again. I'm convinced this Maya situation has made you paranoid. Everybody you meet is either lying or trying to manipulate you now. Pretty soon, you gon' be saying I'm the enemy."

"Just forget it. I'm the crazy paranoid bitch...fine." I shrugged my shoulders, not even wanting to discuss the shit any further.

"Who the fuck is this?" Nico mumbled before answering his cell. "Hello...damn...thanks for letting me know."

"What happened?"

"Another headache. We need to get back to Philly...now!"

Maya

When I checked into my Chairman Suite at the Rittenhouse Hotel, I walked into the marble bathroom, and wondered whether I should take a long bubble bath in the oversized Jacuzzi, or drench myself in the separate shower with massage head. I chose a hot bath, mainly because I wanted to rest my feet. I had been hammering the downtown Philly boutiques all day in my quest to find the perfect outfit to lure Arnez with. I knew the shit wouldn't be easy. The nigga was clearly a seasoned hustler and probably was apprehensive about what chicks he fucked with, so I had to be careful with my attire and approach.

After soaking in the tub for what seemed like at least an hour, I slipped on the plush bathrobe and slippers that the hotel provided, then stood in front of the huge window with a city view. It was amazing how hot Philly looked at night with all the lights shining brightly. I continued to take in the scene and thought how relieved I was to have additional time to plan my shit out. Originally, Arnez was supposed to have lunch at the Lacroix, but then at the last minute the waiter called Steve to let him know that Arnez's bodyguard had cancelled, and wanted to make sure that his regular table would be available for dinner instead. With that happening, it allowed me preparation time I desperately needed, because I always heard that the first impression was the lasting one.

That's why I felt I could make no real headway with Supreme, because he didn't see me as a bona fide woman. He remembered me as Precious' little play sister and Clip's girlfriend. No matter how good I sucked and rode his dick, I wasn't grown and sexy; just a little girl trying to play dress-up. But I refused to give up on my quest to have Supreme as my man, and maybe forging a relationship with Arnez could smooth the progress of that.

I pulled out the Fiesta Red one-shoulder dress I had purchased earlier today. After hours of coming up short, I was ready to give up my search until I hit gold. It was dangling smack in the middle of the high-end Italian boutique's store window. I instantly thought about Precious and the time she said, "If you want to fuck a nigga without giving him no pussy, strut around in his face with a bad ass red dress and he'll do anything to get a taste." I need that shit to work for me tonight.

As I slipped on the dress and the four-inch heels that further accentuated every curve in my body, I thought about how proud Precious would be of me. It was the exact sort of attire she would approve of: giving you the goods without exploiting the goods. As I turned around in the mirror admiring the excellent choice I made, I heard my cell ringing. "What's up, Steve?"

"I hope you're not too far away, because Arnez just got to the restaurant."

"I'm very close. I'm staying at the hotel where the restaurant is at."

"Aren't you a smart girl!"

"I like to think so. So, the waiter is expecting me and will make sure I get a seat near Arnez, correct?"

"Indeed. He is expecting you. He wanted me to ask you what you'll be wearing and how long before you show up."

"He won't be able to miss me. I'll be in a red dress. Tell him I'll be there in fifteen minutes."

"Will do…and be careful."

"Don't worry about me, I'll be perfectly fine. Now, call the waiter and let him know to be looking out for me shortly."

After touching up my makeup and scrutinizing my entire look a few more times to the point that I knew it couldn't get any better, I grabbed my purse and headed out. I strolled down the hallway towards the elevator and noticed a room door slightly open, but nobody came out so I kept on my way, not thinking too much of it. When I turned the corner, I heard a door slam shut. The sound of keys dangling let me know how much closer the person was getting. I hit the down button on the elevator again, because for some reason I was getting an uneasy feeling. When the elevator door opened, I damn near leaped inside. There was a middle aged Asian couple looking at me bizarrely, and they practically jumped to the other side trying to get as far away from me as possible. I couldn't front, my entire vibe was giving off a crazy-chick-up-to-no-good, especially when I diligently kept pushing the button to close the door.

Right when I moved back to the corner to breathe a sigh of relief because the elevator was almost completely shut, a huge hand with long thick fingers latched on to the steel which caused the doors to open right back up. I swallowed hard, about to break out in a sweat. I didn't understand why I was tripping so hard, but the pouncing in my stomach indicating to me that shit was off wouldn't stop.

Oh shit! Maybe Devon's worthless ass got hip to me being in Philly and 'bout to take my ass out right here on this elevator with these Asian motherfuckers watching. Damn, it's gon' be a massacre, 'cause he gon' get ya' too. I started feeling inside my purse. *Oh shit, I ain't even got no heat on me! I'm fucked! Damn, maybe I can grab one of they asses and use them for a shield. Fuck that! I ain't going out like this. This nigga gon' have to come harder than this.*

All this shit was running around in my head, and I was about to snatch the Asian lady since she was the closest to me, but then I caught his face and the fear vanished. The nigga was clean; I mean I'm talking custom designer shit that I wouldn't even know the brand of. It seemed to be tailored to fit his physique, and *his* only. He was in all black, but the richness of the fabric even had the Asian folks sizing him up, like who the fuck is this Negro? Then I caught the blinged out pinky ring. The shit was flashy but classy, and you wouldn't think a ring that big with so many diamonds could be described that way.

When the elevator door opened, I was strongly considering diverting my original plan to seduce Arnez, to get at dude instead. The nigga was so on point that I started thinking about any celebrities I had seen that he might be, but I couldn't think of any, and his hotness superseded theirs anyway. He exuded confidence, which took his sexiness even higher up on the radar. What also intrigued me was that even in my red dress, dude wasn't paying me no mind. It was like he had an agenda, and sniffing after some pussy wasn't on it. I knew I had business to tend to, but was drawn to this man. It was as if I had to know what the fuck he was up to. As I tried to stay out of view but watched his movements, there was something dangerous about his aura too. That also had me open.

I diverted towards the front desk area to make it

look as if I was off his trail, and once he went outside to the front, I quickly went to the glass opening to be nosey. There were three black Yukon's parked behind each other. The mystery man first stopped at the last truck, and the passenger window rolled down. A few words were exchanged, and then the window rolled back up. Then he went to the next truck, and the same exact thing occurred. He finally went to the truck parked in front. A big burly dude stepped out and opened the back door for the mystery man. He got in, and then all three trucks drove off.

I wasn't a psychic, but some shit seemed terribly off to me. That pouncing in the pit of my stomach hadn't left, but I decided there wasn't shit I could do about it, so I continued on to what brought me out to this motherfucker in the first place.

When I entered the restaurant, like I knew it would and should be all eyes were on me. Even the old undercover KKK type motherfuckers were drooling at the mouth, causing their knifed up elderly wives to curl up their lips in disgust.

Right when the hostess was making her way over to greet me, the waiter, who I assumed Steve had put on the payroll, cut in. "Amanda, she'll be dining in my section. I'll seat her," he said, taking the menu from her hand. She gave him a confused stare, but didn't put up a fuss. I gave her a pleasant smile and followed him. "You were supposed to be here fifteen minutes ago," he said, in a lecturing whisper."

"I got a little held up."

"You're lucky we're not swamped tonight or I wouldn't have been able to hold your table." He had somewhat of a diva attitude with him, but I let it slide since his services were needed.

"Sorry, but I'll make sure to leave you a good tip. How 'bout that?" He gave me a gracious smile, so I guess all was good now.

"One table over to your left." He winked, then followed with a, "What can I get you to drink?"

"Bottled water will be fine." I wanted liquor, but I needed to feel the situation out first. It didn't take much to give me a buzz, and I wasn't sure how much work I had to put in to get Arnez's attention.

I looked over at the table the waiter informed me about, and saw Arnez sitting there, having an intense conversation with another gentleman. I then noticed a man standing behind him who I recognized from the pictures Steve showed me as being his bodyguard. I wasn't quite sure how I was going to pull this shit off. He came across just like the man on the elevator; too much business on his mind to think about sniffing after some pussy. The red dress I was rockin' wasn't going to be a powerful enough tool. I needed to be butt-ass naked to pull this shit off.

I ordered some food that I knew I wasn't going to be able to eat, not because I wasn't starving, but figuring out how to maneuver this shit was consuming too much of my energy to devour any food. As the time ran away,

I was coming up short.

I went to the bathroom twice, switching my ass slowly hoping to get a glimmer of his attention, but got nothing. The bodyguard was so in tuned to watching over his boss that he didn't even glance in my direction. A bitch was stuck.

Once my dinner came, I used the fork to play with my food, wishing for a miracle to fall in my lap, but death seemed to land instead. As my mind was wandering about, my eyes fell upon a familiar face. Devon had just entered the restaurant, dressed in all black, and I knew he had come gunning for me. *How did this motherfucker know I was here? Maybe the dude on the elevator really was after me, but was playing it cool so I wouldn't get suspicious. Oh shit, I can't believe it! I have to get the hell out this place, now! There has to be a back way out!*

I turned my face away, hoping that Devon had not yet noticed where I was sitting. At the same time, I was searching for my waiter so he could tell me how to get the fuck outta here. My hands and legs were shaking so badly that my knees were knocking up against the bottom of the table. I didn't see my waiter anywhere, and I didn't know what the fuck to do. I didn't have a weapon on me, so I grabbed at the knife on the table but quickly dropped it, knowing it wouldn't do shit for my cause. My brain was spinning, determined to come up with a plan, and I decided precisely what my next move would be.

I grabbed my purse and slid from my chair, and walked directly up to Arnez's table. His bodyguard moved forward, and Arnez put his hand up as if telling him it was okay. "Yes?" Was the only word he spoke in a calm but firm voice. The man sitting across from him looked up at me, and then back at Arnez.

"Don't make it obvious, but the man standing near the entrance dressed in all black is here to kill you."

"How do you know?"

"Because when I went to the bathroom, I overheard a gentleman on the phone giving a description of a man that needed to be taken out. I didn't realize he was talking about you until I sat down and looked over at your table. You've been warned."

Arnez immediately tapped his bodyguard and nodded his head as if directing him to look forward. From where he was sitting, his view was somewhat obscured, and I guess he needed someone he trusted to legitimize what I said. I slightly turned my head to see if Devon was still standing in the same spot, but to my horror he was coming in my direction, and right beside him was the big burly man who opened the car door for the mystery man I saw on the elevator. *Damn! That nigga brought backup so just in case he missed, somebody else would finish the job. Were the rest of those motherfuckers in them trucks here for me too? Oh shit, I'm fucked!*

As I saw them getting closer, I turned back around to Arnez, and that's when I caught his bodyguard pulling out his metal. At that moment I hit the floor, because I knew in only a matter of seconds it would be on and poppin'.

Less than two seconds after I hit the floor, the man that was dining with Arnez followed my lead, but he was one second late. The bullets I was sure were meant for me caught him instead. His hand was grabbing onto the back of my ankle, and I had to kick my leg to get free as I hauled ass, trying to make an escape. The entire restaurant was in an uproar, as they couldn't believe 'hood violence had made its way to their elite establishment.

The chaos persisted as all the patrons and staff were bolting towards the same exit while trying to dodge bullets. I refused to stand up, preferring to crawl fast and try to stay unnoticed, which I knew would be difficult in a bright ass red dress. I observed a bunch of staff rushing towards the kitchen, so I knew there had to be an exit that way, so I crawled as quickly as I could in that direction. When I made it out, I could hear the mayhem continuing, but my life was still intact and that was all that mattered. So what if innocent people had to die so I could live? It was them or me, and I chose them.

Unsure whether Devon and his people knew what room I was in, I decided not to take a chance and go back inside the hotel. Instead, I ran to the parking garage where my rental car was. I drove slowly around the corner, wanting to see if the cops had made their way to shut shit down, or whether the shootout was still in effect. As I drove closer, I could see that they were already beginning to lock the street down.

While in the process of making a U-turn, from my rearview mirror I could see what looked to be Arnez running down a back street. I figured that the nigga was dead, but since he was still alive, I decided to use it to my advantage. I sped down the street to catch up with him, and the car screeched loudly as I pressed down on the brakes pulling up beside him. He was visibly shaken until I rolled down the window and showed my face. "Get in!" I said, unlocking the door.

At first Arnez hesitated, but then looked back and saw all the police going down the street. I figured after weighing his options, he decided to ride with me.

Precious

The entire ride back to Philly, I kept wondering what the fuck could've happened that we had to leave Brooklyn ASAP. All I knew was that CoCo had placed a call to Nico, but because she was so paranoid about saying certain shit on the phone, she wouldn't give him any details. The most he got out of her was that there had been some major drama, and we needed to come back now.

Before even going back to our hotel, Nico went to a warehouse CoCo told him to meet her at. When we pulled up, I only saw a white Range Rover, which I assumed belonged to her.

Once inside, the huge warehouse had millions of dollars worth of weapons and drugs. *This chick must really trust Nico to bring him here.*

"I hope you didn't have any trouble finding the spot," CoCo said, when she came walking out from a back room.

"No, your directions were on point. So, what the fuck is going on?"

"I know that shit must've been irking the fuck outta you. Driving all the way from New York to here, not knowing what the rush was."

"Pretty much. So, what is it?"

"Last night there was a shootout at this restaurant over there in Center City."

"What!"

"Yeah, that spot at the Rittenhouse Hotel."

"Somebody shot up a restaurant at that joint! Yo, I know them crackers was going crazy up in that motherfucker."

"Damn right!"

"Who were they gunning for?"

"This nigga, Arnez Douglass."

"Why does that name sound so familiar?"

"That's the dude I used to do business with in Atlanta for a while."

"Yeah, that's right! Arnez was a major player."

"Still is, but when shit got hot in ATL, he came to Philly tryna take over."

"Okay, but why is him getting shot at an emergency to me? I don't know that nigga like that."

"Here's the thing. The person responsible is Delondo."

"Delondo! As in the cat Devon works for?"

"That's the one. Devon and one of Delondo's other workers were the two men that went in the spot busting bullets like they were out there in the Wild Wild West. Arnez's bodyguard got killed, and another nigga he was with and one of Delondo's men got killed. The other one is at the hospital in critical condition. I don't know which one is still alive, but if it's Devon, I figured you'd want to try and speak with him about that girl you're looking for in case he don't make it."

Upon hearing this information, all I could do was put my head down. The first time a real lead panned out, this bullshit had to happen.

"Fuck!" Nico yelled out. "Even if he was the one alive, I know there has got to be a cop keeping watch at his door."

"Maybe, but I'm sure that can be handled. I already put in some calls trying to verify who it is at the hospital anyway. But since the shit happened last night and didn't nobody have ID on them, and it ain't like motherfuckers coming forward claiming folks, it's taking a minute to get names and shit."

"So, what the fuck is going on between this nigga, Delondo and Arnez that they bringing gunfire to the Rittenhouse?"

"That nigga, Arnez is a foul motherfucker, do you hear me! He's the one responsible for turning my sister against me. He's also responsible for having Genesis' best friend killed, and we believe his wife also!"

I can't believe Genesis was married and his wife got killed. She must be the mother of his son. Wow, that's some sad shit right there. I ain't feeling that nigga because of that Maya shit, but my heart goes out to him for having to experience that kinda loss.

"Besides the beef we have with him, there is a major turf war going on between Arnez and Delondo, and of course Arnez is the one who started the shit. After Arnez had Delondo's original crew wiped out, Delondo has been determined to finish him off. But Arnez's ass managed to escape death again. I can't wait for that nigga to get his!"

"Damn! Shit is serious out in these streets. I've been on the low for the last couple of months, so I haven't been dealing with the madness, but it's interesting to see what is waiting for me."

"Trust me, I can't wait to break free from this shit. When I got locked up, damn near every dime I had made after all these years of grinding dried up. And the Feds practically wiped Genesis out. If it wasn't for Quentin putting us back on, we would've been fucked up out here. That's why I'm buggin' over how Arnez is maintaining."

"But I remember dude was making serious paper, right?"

"Yeah, but then shit dried up in Atlanta because it got hot there, and then he was doing it big in Philly for a minute. But when Delondo came down from New York, he dominated and froze Arnez up. But somehow, Arnez kept coming up with the cash to stay afloat even in these hard times. If I didn't know better, I would think that he had some sort of connect funneling him paper, but I know all the players that got it like that, and don't none of them fuck wit' Arnez. So, I don't know what the deal is. Maybe in his heyday he was doing way more saving than I gave him credit for."

I couldn't believe how small the motherfuckin' world was. First, there was Mike, then Nico, now I had to add CoCo and Genesis to the ever-expanding list of Quentin Jacobs' dick riders. He had more fans than a pop star. The shit was utterly annoying. Refusing to think about that motherfucker any longer, I had to get back to what was important.

"CoCo!" When I said her name her face look startled, as if she forgot I was in the building or maybe it was because I was loud with it. Plus I had been on mute while she was running off at the mouth. "When can you get that information on Devon? If the nigga is dead, then it doesn't make sense for us to waste any more time in Philly," I said, turning towards Nico. "We need to start coming up with new leads. If he is in the hospital, we need to get to him and not waste any time."

"Let me call one of my street informants now. Maybe some new news came in."

While CoCo was making her call, Nico stepped to me with disillusionment in his eyes. "I can't help but think that maybe if we would've stayed and not gone to New York, we could've got to Devon before all this shit went down."

"I can't front, that very thought went through my mind, but we don't know if he even came back to the address we had on him. For all we know, he could've been stashed some place with Delondo and the rest of his crew, waiting and plotting to take that nigga, Arnez out. Regardless, we did the right thing going to Ms. Duncan's funeral. I would've felt some-kind-of-way if I didn't go and pay my respects. When I was growing up, there were days I woulda went hungry if it wasn't for her. My mother was so busy pulling tricks and smoking that pipe that she didn't give a damn if I was fed or not. You know I want to find Maya's scandalous ass, but that was one stop I would've never forgiven myself for if I hadn't made it."

"I feel you. No matter which way the shit falls, we stay on our hunt. Maya can't hide forever. Eventually, we'll catch her ass."

"Nothing yet. Supposedly the police are keeping information closely guarded. But of course, the minute I find out anything, I'll hit you up," CoCo let us know.

"Do that. We're going back to our hotel. But I'll be waiting to hear from you."

"Cool."

When I woke up, I didn't realize it was the next day until I looked outside and saw it was daylight. When Nico and I got back to the hotel it was early evening, and I only planned on taking a nap, but I guess my body had other ideas. I had to admit, the rest did me some good and I probably needed a lot more of it, but there simply wasn't time.

I looked at my cell to see if I had any missed calls from Nico, but I didn't. I knew that meant he hadn't gotten any new information regarding Devon. If it wasn't for the fact that I hoped he could lead us to Maya, I would've felt justice was served if Devon was deceased, even if it was not by me, but we were placing a lot of stock in him getting us off of our dead end trail.

As I was about to call Nico, to see what he felt should be our next move, my cell started ringing. It was marked private, which I never liked to answer, but very few people had my new number so curiosity got the best of me.

"Hello."

"Good morning, Precious. I hope you slept well."

"Who is this?" The voice had a familiarity to it, but I couldn't place it.

"This is Genesis."

"How did you get this number?"

"I have my ways."

"What do you want?" I asked, not amused by him, or his word usage to play games.

"Can you meet me for breakfast in say...an hour?"

"For what? Last time I saw you, you didn't have too much conversation for me. Has anything changed?"

"I guess there's only one way to find out. Are you going to meet me or not?"

My head wanted to tell the motherfucker hell no, but my mouth said, "Name the spot. I'll be there."

I decided not to tell Nico that I was meeting with Genesis. I hung the Do Not Disturb sign on the doorknob and headed out. I was meeting Genesis at a restaurant that was only a block from the hotel we were staying in, so I figured he somehow knew that information too. He could've easily gotten it from CoCo, as I was sure that Nico had shared it with her.

When I arrived at the cute but tiny location, Genesis was already sitting at a table in the back. He glanced up from what looked to be a newspaper he was reading, and then right back down, not giving me any sort of facial expression. I took a seat, and several seconds passed before he even acknowledged my presence.

"Are you hungry? Because I ordered you something to eat," he said.

"You don't even know what I like."

"I decided to take a chance. Maybe I got it right. But they have the best pancakes in all of Philly, so you'll enjoy them."

"If you say so. But honestly, food isn't on my mind. I want to know why you called me, and what do you want?"

"I wanted to apologize for what happened a few nights ago. I should've been more considerate of your dilemma."

"You could've told me that bullshit on the phone."

He let out a slight chuckle, and then said, "If you

don't mind me asking, how did you meet Supreme, and then get him to marry you? Because you seem like the sort of woman that puts a man through a lot of changes." "If you don't mind me asking, how did you get your wife to marry you? I mean, because you seem like the kind of man that would put your woman through a lot of deadly changes…if you know what I mean."

Dude gave me this ice-cold look, like it was taking all of his strength not to reach over the table and take me out of this world. But that's what the motherfucker got for wasting my time and then talking slick to me about how I got my husband.

"It doesn't feel good, does it? Fuckin' wit' somebody and then they come back and fuck wit' you harder, especially when it gets extremely personal. So, my advice to you is don't play those type of games with me, Genesis. And the reason why is because I know no boundaries."

"No wonder your husband left you and ran off with another woman, because you are a straight up bitch. Right on time! Here's our food. I promise you, you're going to love the pancakes."

This nigga had fuckin' pissed me off, and it wasn't even because of the "bitch" comment. Hell, I was a bitch…the Queen Bitch at that. I wore that title with pride, because it meant don't fuck with me, and don't underestimate me, I run this! It was the part about my husband running off with another woman that had me ready to stab him with my fork. But I knew the fuckin' reason he said that shit was to get under my skin, and I refused to give him the pleasure of seeing it on my face. Yeah, I was human, so he knew in my heart I was hurt behind his statement. But trust, that wasn't enough gratification for a confident nigga like him. He wanted to see me squirm…not! So as my insides burned up in anger, I spread the butter on my hot pancakes, watching as it melted in before pouring the warm syrup over them. Instead of using my fork as a weapon to kill Genesis, I killed my pancakes, slashing through the stack of three, consuming every bite until they were all gone. I then washed it down with a tall glass of orange juice. "You were right. These were the best pancakes I've ever had." I smiled, savoring the fact that I had kept my cool even though inside my rage was boiling over.

"I knew you would enjoy them," Genesis said, returning the smile. "Yes, she's finished with her food. Can you clear her area? Thank you," he instructed the waitress, acting as if he was the consummate gentleman.

"So, now that we've cleared the air and finished eating, why don't you tell me why you really invited me here?"

"I already did. As I stated, I should've been more considerate of your dilemma. I won't make that mistake again. As much as I would love to stay and keep you company further, I have a lot of business to handle today. But I'll be in touch."

Then without any further explanation, Genesis made his exit, and for the first time since I could remember, a man had actually left me in a state of confusion.

Maya

I observed as Arnez was having a telephone conversation with somebody that was causing him to act extra animated. He was pointing his finger midair as if the person was standing in front of him and he was up in their face. Then he pulled the phone away from his ear and looked at it as if he was saying, 'No the fuck you didn't just say that bullshit to me' but whoever he was speaking to, really did, which caused his over-the-top hand gestures to continue.

While I sat on the couch, I tried to pretend that I was all into the Young and the Restless and normally I would be glued. But at this moment, I was straining my ear trying to listen to every word Arnez was spitting out of his mouth. After forty minutes of a heated exchange, he finally ended the call and pounded his fist on the table.

I didn't say shit. I kept pretending that the showdown between Victor and his son Adam had my full attention. "Describe the man you saw when you went to the bathroom."

"Huh?"

"The man you saw on the phone, describe him." I can't front, it took me a minute to process what the fuck Arnez was saying. For one, he hadn't really said more than a couple of words to me since we got to this rundown motel in some backwards ass town in Pennsylvania. Then, I almost forgot my own lie because his question was so fuckin' out the blue it threw me off.

"Oh, you talking about at the restaurant," I said, buying myself some time to conjure up a bullshit description of some fictitious nigga that I didn't see on my way to the restroom. But instead I did what came easier. I described the nigga I was lusting after in the elevator.

"Of course, where else would I be talking about?"

"Don't mind me, I was so caught up in my soap, I wasn't really paying attention to what you said."

"Ok…" he nodded his head but at the same time letting me know to get to it.

"He was medium height and build, maybe a shade darker than you with a low haircut but had waves. He sported a thin mustache and was very well dressed."

"That sound like that nigga Delondo!"

"Who?"

"Delondo…this nigga I'm having some serious

beef wit'. I can't believe that motherfucker had his men come up in the Lacroix blasting like that. But then again it would be the perfect spot to catch me off guard. It would've worked if it hadn't been for you."

I sat silent and baffled for a few. Is he saying what I think he's saying…that the hit was for him? That Devon wasn't even in that spot looking for me he was coming for Arnez. Wow, that is some crazy shit right there. So the dude on the elevator was a nigga named Delondo that Devon was working for? If this is true then shit did work out in my favor because Arnez looking at me like I saved his life and technically I did although initially I was tryna' save my own.

"I'm glad I saved your life but it wasn't my intention to get in the middle of some beef between you and some man."

"Why were you there anyway? I don't remember seeing you with anybody."

"I was visiting from out of town and was supposed to be meeting a friend but at the last minute he couldn't make it. Since I was already at the restaurant and hungry, plus my hotel room was at the Rittenhouse, I figured I should stay and have dinner."

"I'm glad you did, luck was on my side. But I promise you, Delondo won't be so lucky. This the second bodyguard I've lost behind that nigga."

At first I couldn't believe dude was speaking so freely in front of me but then I thought about the circumstances. He almost got killed. He does believe I saved his life.

Then when he was on the street running for cover I gave him a ride. Now we're hauled up in this motel because he's hiding out. He probably needs someone to express his frustrations to and I'm the only outlet he got.

"Listen, I'm happy I was able to help you out but I need to be going. I have a flight to catch and I need to get back to my hotel." What I was saying was a bunch of bullshit but the nigga could never know that I had actually tracked him down and I was exactly where I wanted to be. As long as I played the role of wanting to get away from his ass I shouldn't raise any suspicion.

"You can't leave."

"Excuse me?"

"I need you to stay here, you have a car."

"I'll drop you off wherever you want to go. I'm sure you have friends in Philly."

"In the business I'm in, I don't have friends only business associates and people that work for me. But after last night, I don't know who is looking out for me or who might hand me over to Delondo. Until I figure it out, I need to keep a low profile. That's why I had you bring me to this motel."

"What business are you in?" I asked, playing naïve.

"Put it this way...a very dangerous one."

"I figured that much after what happened but I didn't want to jump to any conclusions."

"I like to say I'm in the import and export business."

"Of drugs I suppose?"

"Listen, I'll make your time worthwhile. You'll be

well compensated. I just need you to stay put for a minute until I figure out my next move." *Nigga please…I ain't going nowhere. Trust me on that.*

"How long are you talking about? I don't want my family to worry."

"Give me a couple of days," he said shaking his head. "Damn, I need Chanel right now."

"Who is Chanel…is she your girlfriend?"

"She was my everything but she was taken out my life too." I wasn't sure what he meant by that. I mean did she leave him or was the bitch dead? But I decided not to pry. I had the feeling that if I played it cool, the longer I stayed around the nigga, the more information he would voluntarily share.

Ring…ring…ring

"Yo, did you get my message?" I heard Arnez say to whoever was on the other end of the phone. But I was pissed because I couldn't hear what the other person was saying.

"He had his people come at me."

The person on the other end must've said Delondo's name because then Arnez answered, "Yep."

Arnez then stood up from the bed and walked to the bathroom and shut the door. That was one conversation he didn't want me hearing and I was vexed! I was tempted to press my ear against the door to listen but if I got caught then whatever little trust he had for me at the moment would go right out the window. I paced the small area hoping to come up with an idea to get information I wanted on Supreme from Arnez. I also needed to find out what was going on with Devon. Even if he didn't come up in the restaurant to kill me, our eyes locked briefly last night so I know he saw me. If he wasn't looking for me before he would definitely be on the prowl for me now. While considering my options Arnez came busting out the bathroom door interrupting my thoughts.

"Come on, I need for you to take me somewhere," he stated in a rushed tone.

"Where are we going?"

"I'll tell you when we get in the car." I grabbed my purse and headed out. His purposeful strides to the car let me know that wherever we were going he wanted to get there quickly.

"Do you know how to get back to Philly?"

"Yes."

"Good, once you get there I'll tell you where to go."

When I pulled out the parking lot, Arnez's cell phone started ringing.

"Yo' I'm on my way. I should be there in about an hour," he said, then ended the call.

"Where am I taking you?"

"Just drive." *What the fuck have I got myself into? Excitement is good but only when I know what the hell is going on. But right now even though I was driving, Arnez was in complete control and that shit had me antsy.*

As I continued to drive, making my way towards

Philly, Arnez's phone kept blowing up. That shit had to ring at least every couple minutes. Some calls he took, others he ignored. But every time the phone would ring I couldn't help but wonder if Supreme was on the other end of the call.

"Get over to your right. We're getting off at the next exit," he informed me a few minutes after entering Philly. "And when you get off, veer to your left." I followed his directions anxious to see where the final destination would be. "Turn right at the next light...keep going straight... okay slow down. You're about to make this left."

"Into the hospital?"

"Yes, and park right over there." Arnez pointed towards a somewhat discreet area.

"What are we doing at the hospital?"

"Remember I said you would be well compensated for your help."

"Yeah, but what help do you need from me at the hospital?" Arnez pulled out a small piece of paper from his pants pocket and unfolded it.

"I want you to go inside and ask what room," he glanced back down at the paper, "that Devon McNeil is in. Tell them you're his sister and he was shot last night." I couldn't believe that Arnez had led me right to my enemy. If he only knew I would gladly try to find out this information for free.

"I can do that. Hopefully whoever is at the front desk won't put me through a bunch of changes to get the information."

"Just go in there and be convincing. If you get it, it'll be some of the easiest money you've ever made."

"Who is this Devon guy to you…is he a friend of yours?" I already knew the answer to that was hell no but I wanted to see what Arnez would reveal.

"No, he's one of Delondo's men, the one that survived the shooting. I need to know his condition." *So do I*, I said to myself.

"Okay, I'll try to find out everything I can. I'll be back."

As I walked towards the hospital entrance I peeped a few people ogling me strangely and I was trying to figure out what the fuck was wrong with them. Then I looked down and I don't know how I could forget that I had on my fuckem' dress. This bright red shit was hot for a night of seduction but for a daylight hospital visit, it was a tad inappropriate. I could either feel like a fool coming up in the hospital looking like a high priced hooker or I could use the outfit to my advantage.

When I walked in, I stood to the side for a minute and observed the staff. I sized everybody up and saw a younger woman who seemed to be about to start her shift. I waited a couple more minutes for her to get a little situated and for some of the other staff who had probably been there for awhile to get out her face. Once the traffic seemed to be dispersing I made my move.

"Excuse me Miss."

"Yes, can I help you," she said trying not to noticeably stare me up in my outfit.

"I hope so. I've been here all night. I haven't even had a chance to go home. My brother was brought in here last night because he got shot. I was trying to find out if his condition had improved. The woman who I spoke to earlier told me to come back and she would see if there were any updates."

"He came in last night…you said he is your brother?" I nodded my head yes, trying to give off a real gloomy mood. "What's his name?"

"Devon McNeil.'"

"And what's your name?"

"Tawana McNeil."

"He's still in critical condition."

"Have they moved him to another room?"

"I don't know, I just got here but he's in room 302. Is that the same room?"

"Yes, I was checking because they said they might have to move him."

"That was probably if his condition had changed."

"Yeah, that makes sense. Well, thank you for your help."

"No problem."

I turned around and a huge grin crossed my face. Critical condition was good but I needed Devon to be dead and I had a feeling Arnez wanted the same thing. I left the hospital anxious to share the inside scoop with him. I knew he would be pleased and I couldn't wait to find out how he planned on utilizing the information.

As I got closer to the car, I realized Arnez wasn't

inside. I looked around but didn't see him. "Where did he go?" I asked out loud. I kept walking towards the car and halfway there shit seemed to come to a halt and then transition to a movie scene clip.

"Get dooooooown!" I heard what sounded like Arnez's voice yell out. I turned around towards the sound of his voice and that's when I locked eyes with my worst nightmare. She was a few hundred feet away but even from the long distance, it was no doubt the image of Precious Cummings speeding towards me with her gun already raised. I was in complete shock, to the point that I couldn't move. My feet were cemented to the ground. I could hear the *pop…pop…pop* and if it wasn't for Arnez throwing me down to the ground. At least one of those bullets would've ripped through me.

"Come on…come on…come on…" he screamed in my ear, trying to snap me out my daze. He damned near dragged me to the car and threw me in. Precious was getting closer and closer and I couldn't tell if the sound of her gun blasting off was louder, or my heart thumping. One thing I did know though was Arnez was a pro. We were in broad daylight being shot at but the nigga was completely focused. After tossing me in the car his hands didn't shake once as he put the keys in the ignition. The closer Precious got the calmer he seemed to get. Once he started the engine he put it in drive and slammed down on the gas, making a beeline straight towards Precious. She busted off a couple more shots before jumping out the way to avoid being ran over by

Arnez. Before the car was out of view, I turned to face her and our eyes met one final time. Precious' fierce glare said it all. The bitch was back and out for my blood.

Precious

"Yo, are you fuckin' crazy! Get in the car!" Nico, yelled out as he pulled up beside me. I jumped inside and slammed the door. "I can't believe your crazy ass is busting bullets in the fuckin' parking lot of a hospital! You better be lucky there weren't any cops around or we would both be in jail," Nico barked, speeding off and checking in his mirror making sure no cops were on his back.

"I was this close to getting that heffa," I said, pounding my fist in the palm of my hand. That low-life ho is in Philly…ain't that some shit. I bet you she was coming to the hospital to see Devon. But how the fuck she know he was here?" I was running off at the mouth extra amped up. Seeing Maya for the first time in so long had my adrenaline pumping.

"We can't even go inside the hospital and try to speak with Devon now! Them motherfuckers probably got that shit on camera."

"What the fuck was I supposed to do, let her get away?"

"I understand you pumped and seeing Maya got you all riled up but you can't do sloppy shit like that. You got a child to think about. We got the evidence we need to make sure she spends the rest of her life in jail. If we can take her out and get away wit' it cool...otherwise we do it the legal way and make sure she get locked up. But running 'round here playing vigilante in broad daylight is not the move."

I knew Nico was right but I let my emotions get the best of me. When CoCo gave us the information on Devon I couldn't get to the hospital fast enough. Learning he wasn't dead and there was a chance that he could deliver some much needed 411 on Maya had me excited. Nico and I decided I should go in first and try to maneuver my way in Devon's room. So when I got out the car and noticed a woman in a bright red dress coming out the hospital, even from the far distance I knew it was Maya. All reasonable thinking escaped me within seconds.

"I wonder who that dude was with her. I guess one good thing, it damn sure wasn't Supreme. Do you think Maya is up here with Devon?"

"I don't know. All this shit is getting more and more confusing. The only person that can probably give us some answers is Devon. Maybe I can go back to the hospital by myself and try to speak with him."

"That probably would be best. Because you're right, we don't know if anybody saw me turning that parking lot out and we def' don't need the drama."

"Okay, so I'ma drop you back off at the hotel and then head back to the hospital. But Precious I want you to stay in your hotel room and wait for me. Please don't just start lurking the streets in search of Maya."

"I'm not, plus her scared ass probably someplace hiding right now. I can't believe how close I was to ending her life."

"You need to be thanking God that you didn't because if you had, on everything, you would be in handcuffs right now facing murder charges."

As much as I wanted Maya dead spending the rest of my life behind bars wasn't worth it. Aaliyah would grow up without her mother so my revenge would be in vain. I had to be smart about this shit. If I could murder her ass on the low and get away with it then that was mos def' option number one. But anything short of that meant all I could do was give her a good old fashion ass whooping before I let the authorities toss her in jail.

"You're right and I'ma act accordingly. Getting Maya off the streets and out of my life is what's most important."

"I hope you mean that, Precious, because we talking about not only your life but that of your daughter. This shit..." Right when Nico sounded as if he was about to go into a full fledge lecture I heard his cell phone ringing. I was ecstatic because I respected that he was kicking real shit but I didn't want to hear it. The hatred I had for Maya ran so deep that it was almost blinding. If I didn't have my daughter to live for there was a very good chance I would be willing to spend the rest of my life in jail just for the pleasure of killing her myself and watching as she begged to live.

"We're on our way right now," I caught Nico say before getting off the phone.

"You're not about to drop me off at the hotel so you can go to the hospital?"

"No, that was CoCo and she told us to meet her at the warehouse now."

"I wonder what the fuck done happened now. This shit need to be quick because you need to go speak with Devon."

"CoCo said it's important. And she understands the magnitude of shit that's going down right now, so if she's telling us to come, it's must be some serious shit."

When Nico pulled up to the warehouse I saw the white Range Rover, which I knew belonged to CoCo but there was also a cream Bentley but I had no idea who owned that. When we got inside the first person we saw was Genesis so I assumed that Bentley was his shit. I didn't tell Nico about the breakfast I had with Genesis earlier this morning and I still had no desire to. Mainly because

I felt he was purposely trying to play me out and I until I figured out why I was going to keep my feelings to myself, especially since it seemed Nico actually liked the nigga.

"What's up man," Nico said, shaking Genesis' hand. "Good to see you again."

"Likewise, and how are you, Precious?" he asked in an almost condescending tone but I was sure that shit went right over Nico's head.

"The same."

"Where's CoCo, she called and told me it was important we get right over here."

"She's in the back on the phone. I actually just got here myself."

"I don't mean to rush her, but I'm trying to get over to the hospital and see if I can get any information from Devon about Maya. We actually ran into her at the hospital."

"You ran into Maya?" Genesis questioned.

"Yeah, but I'm sure you would have no interest in that since you don't even know who Maya is," I cut in and said, taking a jab at Genesis, letting him know I knew he was full of shit. But he didn't flinch instead he carried on with his conversation with Nico until CoCo came out.

"Sorry I kept you waiting but I was trying to get all the details together before you got here."

"What details?" Nico wanted to know and so did I.

"Devon is dead."

"What!" I swung passed Genesis' wanting to knock him out my way. "We just left the hospital less than an hour ago."

"Well whoever killed him must've done it around that time or close to it because he's dead."

"What do you mean whoever killed him?" Nico took the words right out of my mouth, because I was perplexed by that statement.

"There was supposed to be a guard in front of Devon's room door but somebody got to him. They came in, put a pillow over his head and popped one bullet through his face. By the time the nurses came in the perpetrator was long gone. My sources are telling me Arnez is behind the hit. You know, sending a message to Delondo that you took my man now I've taken both of yours."

"This is too fuckin' much! Devon was supposed to tell us where Maya might be or where she had been so I could find my husband and daughter! Now that motherfucker is dead and I had that hussy within my reach and lost her ass. This shit is beyond fucked up!"

"Your husband…I had no idea you were married," CoCo made known. I glanced at Nico and then at Genesis because for some reason I assumed that at least one of them had told her, but apparently I was wrong.

"Yes, my husband is Supreme, and Maya has damn near single-handedly destroyed my marriage."

"Supreme…is that like a street name or are you talking about 'The Supreme'", CoCo stressed wanting clarification.

"She's talking about 'The Supreme'", Genesis said,

taking it upon himself to answer for me.

"Rapper turned music mogul Supreme," she continued as if she needed further confirmation.

"What, you know the nigga…yes that Supreme!" I was already in a foul fuckin' mood and this chick triple asking me the same question wasn't helping my cause.

"No, I don't know him," she snapped. "I'm surprised that's all. I mean it seems somebody would've told me that you were his wife."

"Well now you know but it don't change shit. Devon is still dead and Maya is still missing. We back at the starting point but I don't even know where the finish line is anymore."

"Precious, I know shit seems a bit bleak right now, but I promised you I would get you home to your daughter and I will." Nico's words were so sincere but I needed more than that to get back to my family. I saw him pull CoCo to the side and I figured he was picking her brain trying to get all the details on what went down with Devon, hoping it could help locate Maya. But I was stuck on the fact that Maya was almost mine but I let her get away. I know I didn't technically let her get away but no matter which way I flipped it she was gone and I was no closer to finding Supreme and Aaliyah.

"Precious, can I speak with you?" I heard Genesis but wasn't in the mood to lift my head up and acknowledge his request. I wasn't mentally up to partake in the game I was for sure he wanted to play. But being the relentless nigga that he is, he chose to ignore my stay-the-fuck-away-from-me body language. "I think you'll want to hear what I have to say."

"I doubt it, but umm, you're not giving me much of a choice are you?"

"Your husband and daughter are in Miami. I have their last known address and I believe it's still good." My mouth dropped when I heard those words come out of Genesis' mouth. This man continued to shock me and now I was speechless which was a rarity for me. I almost wanted to believe he was playing a sick joke on me because to find out Genesis was telling the truth would bring me happiness, a feeling that I had been deprived of for so long.

"Is this real? I mean is what you're saying to me true?" I knew Genesis could see the pleading in my eyes of putting all my hope in what he said.

"It is true. I'ma give you the address to where they are living in Miami and I hope you can work things out with your husband."

"Why...why are you giving me this information now?"

"My wife was taken out of my life and my son will grow up without ever knowing what an incredible woman his mother was. There's nothing I can do to change that but I can change this. Go get your daughter, love her and be the best mother you can possibly be."

"I'll never forget that you did this for me...thank you." As Genesis wrote down the address instead of rejoicing my mind speculated on what this man's agenda was. I didn't doubt he genuinely wanted me to reconnect with my daughter but I was absolutely positive he was hiding a huge piece of the puzzle from me and I needed answers. But for now it would have to wait. I was booking a one-way flight to Miami determined to be reunited with my family.

Maya

"Who was that woman and why was she trying to kill you?" When Arnez asked me that question we had reached a fork in the road. My choice was to either come clean or lie. So I decided to do what I do best.

"I made the mistake of getting involved with this man and he lied to me. He never told me he was married. I only found out recently and that's why I came to Philly so I could end it once and for all. He was the friend that I told you I was supposed to meet at the restaurant. But somehow his wife got my cell number and she called threatening me, it got crazy. We decided it was best he didn't come."

"So how do you think she knew you were going to be at the hospital?"

"That's what I'm tryna figure out, unless it was just crazy coincidence."

"It's a possibility but she came prepared."

"You ain't lying. If you hadn't been there I would be dead right now."

"Saving your life was the least I could do because you did save mine."

"Now we're even. You don't owe me anything."

"If it wasn't for me making you go to the hospital and get that information for me then that man's wife would've never had the opportunity to try and kill you."

"You didn't make me do anything. I wanted to help you."

"And you did, more than you know."

"Where are we going?" We had been driving for awhile but playing out the episode that had went down with Precious over and over again in my head had made me oblivious that I didn't know where the fuck we were going.

"Why, are you ready to go back home?"

"No, I really don't have anything to go back home to. But if you don't need me anymore, you can take me back to my hotel."

"What if I told you that I wanted you to stay?"

"I would ask you why?"

"Because I think you have a lot of heart. When you heard that conversation about what was about to happen you didn't have to warn me, you could've walked out and went about your life. Then I asked you to go in the hospital and get that information for me. You did it with no problem. Most females would be too scared to do what you did but like I said you showed a lot of heart. I appreciate that quality in a woman."

"I'm surprised a man like you doesn't already have a woman like that."

"I did and she was a true soldier."

"Was it that woman you mentioned earlier?"

"Yes, Chanel."

"What happened?"

"Life...life happened. As you know by now danger surrounds me and it seems to surround you too," he remarked, glancing over at me. "It's different circumstances but danger is danger. Unfortunately the danger finally caught up to Chanel."

"You see soldier potential in me?"

"I see something...what, only time will tell. That's why I want you to stay so I can observe you, watch how you move."

"What if I don't have any interest in being your soldier?"

"If that was the case, you wouldn't have stuck around but you're still here."

"I'll tell you what, I'll stay but only if you promise we don't have to go back to that awful motel."

"You don't have to worry about that. Trust me, it was harder on me than it could ever be on you. Living extremely comfortable is all I know." *Shit motherfucker, me too.* But Arnez didn't need to know all that. If a hustler knows a woman is accustomed to the good life the first thing they want to know is how and who got you like that. I never forgot Mike taught me that. He said it was their way of knowing how many times you'd been around the block or if you were fresh meat. Most top-notch hustlers preferred fresh meat and if you had been broken in, anything more than twice was considered damaged goods. They could still fuck around with you but wife you was a no go.

"That's good to hear but I still need to get my stuff from the hotel."

"When are you due to check out?"

"Monday."

"That gives us two more days."

"What about clothes? I'm ready to burn this red dress."

"Don't do that, it looks good on you."

"Really, I didn't' think you noticed."

"I'm a man aren't I, of course I noticed."

"Well, thank you but I'm ready to take this shit off."

"I understand. I'm ready to take these clothes off too. Wearing the same thing two days in a row isn't cool. We're almost in Jersey. When we get there we'll stop at the mall, get a couple of things and then find a hotel. Does that sound like a plan?"

"Yep, sounds like a very good plan to me."

It was amazing what some shopping could do for a bitch. After hitting up The Mall at Short Hills, I felt like

I was gettin' my sexy back. I went from feeling like the broke-down ho Julia Roberts in Pretty Woman, when she was strolling Rodeo Drive trying to spend up all of Richard Gere's money but nobody would give her play. To the new and improved hooker after Mr. Gere personally accompanied Julia on a shopping spree and everybody kissed her ass. Yep, this was exactly what I needed particularly since Supreme had been treating me like some washed up pussy he was done fucking with for the last couple months. Although Arnez hadn't made any sort of sexual advances towards me, being treated to an afternoon of shopping instead of the on-call babysitter had me feeling like a young, desirable woman again.

So when we went to check in to our hotel and Arnez was going to get us separate rooms, I shut that shit down.

"Two suites please."

"Arnez, you don't have to get me a suite."

"I know, but I want to. If I'm gonna be staying in a suite then you should too. I told you, I like only the best."

"I understand that and I appreciate it but what I mean is that, I don't want my own suite. I want to stay with you."

"You know you don't have to do this. Because I took you shopping doesn't mean I expect sex from you. Trust me, it's not that serious."

"I don't do anything I don't want to do."

Arnez gave me the most alluring smile and then said to the lady working behind the front desk, "That'll be one suite."

When Arnez closed the door to our hotel room, my tongue was down his throat before he could even put down the key. I was craving for a touch of a man and some dick. I thought Arnez was the perfect fit. His strong arms cupped my ass and lifted me up off the floor, carrying me over to the king sized bed. I tugged at his shirt and pants simultaneously feeling like a dog in heat. I kissed, licked and bit on his neck and chest. The faint scents of his cologne still lingering in his skin making me crave him that much more.

"Damn baby, you want the dick like that," Arnez whispered in my ear.

"Yes, yes baby, I do," I purred back. So when Arnez finally entered me, I welcomed the warmth as my walls surrounded his thickness. He rocked inside of me taking it deep and then pulling back to the very tip so I could beg for the dick to be back inside. Arnez was no doubt skilled in the technique of fucking because although I knew he had absolutely no love for me, that nigga worked his tool like I was the only woman in the world for him, so at that moment I did feel like we were in love.

Precious

"Precious, I don't want you to worry. I already got the private investigator on it to follow up on some other leads and CoCo is…"

"Nico, stop."

"Stop, I know you don't want to give up because we can't!"

"It's not that."

"Then what?"

"I know where Supreme and Maya are." Nico slammed down on his brakes so hard it caused my body to jerk forward then back. Luckily we were on an isolated back street and no other vehicles were behind us or shit would've been ugly.

"What the fuck are you talking 'bout and when did

you get that information and why are you just now telling me?"

"If you would slow down with all the questions I'll tell you!"

"I'm listening." Nico parked the car on the corner block and stared at me still gripping the steering wheel.

"When you were in the warehouse talking to CoCo, Genesis told me."

"What! Come the fuck again!"

"I told you he knew much more than what he was letting on but right now that's not important. What is important is that he gave me the address to where Supreme and Aaliyah are living. They're actually in Miami."

"Miami, wow…Miami," Nico repeated as if digesting what I told him.

"I can't believe after all this time we've found them…I mean Genesis found them."

"Nico, you deserve a lot of credit too. I didn't even want to come to fuckin' Philly! I wanted to stay in Atlanta, so if we hadn't come here we would've never had met Genesis to get the information. Everything happens for a reason."

"Precious, you don't have to try and stroke my ego. I'm happy you finally found your family. I don't care who gave you the information."

"It's not about stroking your ego. I want you to know how appreciative I am for riding this shit out with me. I know I've been a real pain but you stuck it out and I know you would've went to the end of the world with me if need be and I love you for that."

"So when are you going to Miami?"

"I'm taking the first flight out in the morning."

"Do you need me to come with you?"

"Under the circumstances, I don't think that would be a good idea."

"You're right. I guess after being with you every day for the last few months has made it hard for me to want to let you go. But then again, why lie to myself. I'll never be able to let you go."

"But how selfish am I because I don't want you to be able to let me go." In my heart I didn't. I was married to another man and I loved Supreme more than anything but I loved Nico too. And although I had found happiness with another man I didn't want Nico to find that same happiness with another woman. He had been my crutch for so long that to accept anything differently wasn't an option for me. But I had to let go, because Nico was my past and Supreme was my future.

"Thank you for taking me to the airport."

"I had to make sure you got on the airplane safely. I wouldn't be able to ease my mind if I didn't."

"So what are you gonna do now?"

"I'ma stay in Philly a few more days. I have a lot of business to discuss with CoCo and Genesis. We're going to try and collaborate on some shit."

"I think that's a good idea. Even though I was right about Genesis knowing more than what he was telling me, I think you was right about him too. He's a decent dude. I have no doubt the three of you can make a shit load of money together." Nico and I both smiled at the same time. "I really do love you." I knew I shouldn't have said that but I couldn't help myself.

"I know and I love you too. But you're right, you belong with Supreme." I nodded my head in agreement.

"But listen, you need to catch your flight. We've come too far for you to miss it. And listen, no worries I'll still find Maya. The evidence we have against her is safely put away and I promise she'll never be able to hurt you and your family again."

"Okay. I'll call you when I get to Miami. Wish me luck!"

"You don't need it," Nico grinned before kissing me on my forehead and walking off. To watch him leave brought a deep sadness in my heart. Part of me hated that I loved him so much but the other part wouldn't want to change that for nothing in the world. I took a deep breath ready for the next chapter in my life…going home to my family.

When my flight landed at the Miami International Airport my emotions were mixed. I would be able to hold my daughter after being away from her for so long but

I was scared about the reception I would receive from Supreme. I wasn't expecting him to welcome me with open arms but I hoped that he would at least hear me out, I deserved that—we deserved that. During my taxi ride, I continued to think of different scenarios of how it would all play out and I had to admit, my nerves were getting the best of me.

"Are we almost there?" I asked realizing we had now entered a residential area with elegant mansions and riverfront estates situated on high bluffs overlooking pools and terraced grounds.

"Yes only a few more minutes," the taxi driver informed me. He continued to drive and when he started to slow down and look around I knew we were getting near. "We're here," he said, making a right into a driveway with open gates. I saw a fuchsia Ferrari parked in the circular entrance and I hoped that meant Supreme was home.

"Beautiful home…here take my card. Call if you ever need a ride." I reluctantly took his card but hoping never to need his services again. I grabbed the one bag I had and stepped out the taxi. It took me a couple of seconds to close the door as I stood staring at the entrance until finally slamming it shut ready to face my fears.

It felt like I was moving in slow motion as I made my way to the front door. I swallowed hard before ringing the doorbell. It was like déjà vu from when I rang the doorbell at our home in Beverly Hills and my world was shattered when I realized I had returned to nothing. That couldn't happen to me again. I wouldn't be able to handle it. Not getting an answer, I rang the doorbell again and pounded on the door no longer afraid but determined. As the door opened I stepped forward and when my eyes met with Supreme's a natural reflex kicked in. I dropped my bag on the front step and wrapped my arms around his neck pulling his mouth to mine. His lips and tongue gave into mine and for a few minutes the passion the connection was strong. Our love was intact as if we had never been apart. Then the fantasy vanished and reality was ready to kick my ass.

"It would be nothing for me to kill you right now!" Supreme roared, wrapping his hands around my neck and slamming me against the wall in the foyer. I was trying to speak but he was choking me and I wasn't even able to gasp for air. He was doing all this with the front door still wide open, not giving a fuck who witnessed it. I quickly began feeling light headed as his grip became tighter. It was like Supreme was trying to break my neck off. The bulging of my eyes must've made him realize the severity of his actions because right when I thought it was about to be lights out, he released me from his clutch as my body hit the cold marble floor.

As if an afterthought, Supreme slammed the door shut and walked right over me leaving me right where I was. I was gasping for air trying to figure out how I went to passionately kissing my husband to laying on the floor grateful to be alive. I watched as Supreme disappeared into what appeared from where I was positioned to be the living room. While getting my bearings together I thought about how quiet the house was and wondered where Aaliyah was and would she remember me.

I got my strength together and headed in the direction I saw Supreme go. He was sitting on the couch having a drink. He had to know it was too early in the morning for that shit but clearly he didn't give a fuck. But after almost killing your wife, I supposed he would need to drink something powerful. I too needed a drink, I went over to the bar and poured myself a glass of water.

"Where's Aaliyah?"

"Did you really think you could come here and I would just fuckin' greet you wit' open arms," he barked ignoring my question. "Do you even know how much I hate you!" he screamed throwing his half filled glass of liquor as it shattered against the fireplace.

"Please hear me out. If you would listen to me, you'll realize we've both been taken on a fuckin' rollercoaster ride." I was trying to remain calm because one of us had to if we were going to make any progress. If both of our tempers were flaring the dark place we were already in would only go deeper.

"What...listen to your lies and try to dig yourself out the hole you dug! Get the fuck outta here! I would rather you tell me the truth so I can fuckin' hate you for the rest of my life!"

"Oh you want to hate me...how 'bout I want to hate you too for not believing in our love and that I would never abandon you and Aaliyah! Or how 'bout I want to hate you for fuckin' Maya! But as much as I want to hate you I can't because I fuckin' love you too much!"

"How do you know about me and Maya?" that was the first question Supreme asked me in a normal tone instead screaming and yelling.

"She told me."

"When did you talk to Maya?"

"When she had me chained up, held hostage in the house with Mike."

"What?" Supreme stood up pacing back and forth for a moment and raising his arms in confusion. "I don't understand," he continued pressing his fingers against his temples.

"Let me help clear it up for you. Maya played me for months, hell it might've been years...I don't know. What I do know is after Mike got locked up for rapping me she plotted with him to break him out of jail, have it appear like Clip was the one behind everything so she could get rid of me and have you and my life for herself."

"This don't even sound plausible. It sounds like some outlandish made-for-TV movie. Is this the best lie you could come up with to excuse you leaving your family to run off with Nico!"

"Look at me!" Now screaming running up on Supreme. "Look at me!" I screamed louder, grabbing his arm turning him to face me. "Look at me!" I bolted again, now at the top of my lungs pointing my fingers towards my eyes, emphasizing my face. "I would never leave you or Aaliyah for Nico or any other man! You look at me and tell me you don't believe me because I know in your heart you do. That day I thought you died in my arms I didn't want to live anymore."

"It didn't stop you from fuckin' Nico when you thought my body was still cold."

I put my head down in shame for a moment because I did regret Supreme ever found out about that. "I thought you were dead. I know that doesn't change the pain you feel for finding that out but I was completely lost without you and I needed to feel connected to somebody."

"So the man who left you for dead and killed our unborn child was the person who was able to do that for you."

"Supreme, don't do this. There is nothing I could ever say that would make my relationship with Nico sound sane."

"Because it isn't sane! The shit is sick!"

"That could very well be true but it doesn't change the fact that I chose you. Nico was never an option, it was always you."

"What about the letter. You wrote that."

"Maya forced me to. She threatened to harm Aaliyah if I didn't. If you only knew the torture I went through behind that conniving bitch!"

"How was Maya able to pull all this shit off by herself?"

"She had help. For one, Devon."

"Devon McNeil the bodyguard that worked for me?"

"Yes that Devon."

"What! This is getting more bizarre by the minute."

"Well get ready for this...it was Maya who killed Mike."

"Her brother...Maya killed her own brother?"

"Yes, Mike wanted to let me live and help me get Aaliyah and of course Maya couldn't let that happen. She was using our daughter to get close to you. I forgive you, Supreme. I need for you to know that. I forgive you for unwillingly being a part of her manipulation and ultimately giving into temptation by having sex with her." He turned towards me and then looked away. "Devon held me as Maya beat me unmercifully, leaving me for dead before she burned the house down."

As if Supreme couldn't stand to hear anymore he collapsed on the couch and buried his face in his hands. But I refused to let up. If I wanted my husband back, which I did, he needed to believe every word I was saying. I couldn't leave a doubt in his mind that my story was nothing short of a hundred percent truth.

"When I was being held captive, Maya ripped off the pink diamond necklace you gave me. I guarantee you somewhere in this house with her belongings she has it. That necklace represented a symbol to her that she ripped us apart and that she won." Supreme lifted his head up and stared at me and for the first time I could see regret as his eyes watered up.

"How can you ever forgive me? I want to say sorry but it sounds like such a baby word right now. I was sleeping with the enemy all that time. I let her take care of our daughter." Misery flooded Supreme's face and my heart broke for him. I knew I could forgive him but the real question was would Supreme be able to forgive himself.

Maya

Being with Arnez for the last few days gave me a different view on my relationship with Supreme or lack thereof. When Arnez was inside of me I could feel how much he wanted me and desired my body. With Supreme it always felt as if there was someplace he'd rather be or better yet someone else he would rather be with. I wasn't ignorant to the fact his preference was Precious but I had convinced myself if I put it on him just right his wife would eventually become an afterthought. With all the time and energy I put into making Supreme mine I wasn't ready to abandon my plan just yet. While Arnez was out, I decided to call him and see if my absence had made him miss me at all.

I rocked my leg back and forth sitting on the edge

of the bed waiting for Supreme to answer the phone. "Hello." When a female voice answered his phone I instantly hit the end key. I waited a few seconds and called right back thinking maybe I dialed the wrong number but the same voice answered and I didn't want to believe it was who it sounded like.

"Who is this?"

"Precious Mills. Who is this?" I was silent not knowing what to say. "Is this Maya?" Precious asked without hesitation. "Why don't you speak the fuck up? I know that's yo' sorry ass on the other end of this phone. Yeah, heffa I'm back and Supreme know everything!"

"You'll pay for this, Precious."

"Ho, I've already paid. The fact that I know you was fucking my husband is payment enough. But we good now. And trust, I got something for yo' sneaky ass. Wherever you at, whatever you doing, enjoy this little bit of freedom while you can, because baby girl your days are up. Now get the fuck off my husbands' phone!"

The line went dead but I was still holding the phone in an attempt to convince myself the conversation that took place hadn't.

"The other day Precious was in the parking lot in Philadelphia unloading her weapon on me and now she was answering Supreme's phone, how the hell did that happen? I laid up in the bed with Arnez for a few days and my entire life has changed," I stated out loud in bewilderment. I fell back on the bed, stunned by the turn of events. What really had me confused was how Precious was able to find Supreme. He had done everything to make sure Precious couldn't track him down but there she was back on her throne. All I could do was scream at the top of my lungs and punch the pillow on the bed as if I was beating the shit out of Precious.

Knock…knock…knock

"Is everything alright in there?" I heard the cleaning lady ask through the door.

"Sorry 'bout that. Everything's fine. I accidentally ripped a dress I was putting on and got upset," I lied. Precious had my mind in another world that I forgot I was in a hotel. This wasn't the time for me to lose my mind if anything I needed to come up with a new game plan and fast. My cover was officially now blown and I wasn't sure what Precious' next move would be. Would she turn me into the police for kidnapping and the murder of my brother, Clip and a few other folks? If she did, would they even believe her story. With Devon dead who could corroborate the shit.

On the other hand, Precious wasn't exactly the fuck with the police type. There was an excellent chance she would decide to get that street justice, which meant I would be looking over my shoulder for the rest of my life. Either way the dice weren't rolling in my favor and I was fucked. I had to come up with a way to get back in the driver's seat. My brain was going in deep scheme mode when I heard Arnez using his key to open the door.

Normally I would welcome his company but I couldn't think about dick right now. This was about life, death, freedom or jail.

"I thought you would be dressed by the time I got back," were the first words out of Arnez's mouth when he saw me.

"I slept late."

"We need to be heading out, we have a busy day."

"When you say heading out are you talking about leaving for good?"

"Yep. We have to stop in New York for a day then head back to Philly. Things have gotten somewhat calmer so it's time for business as usual."

"What are we going to New York for?"

"Business and pleasure."

"What sort of pleasure?"

"There's a party going on tonight that I need to attend."

"I'm not in the mood for a party tonight. Would you mind if I didn't go?"

"Of course I would mind. This wasn't a request. You will be attending this party with me. I've already picked out what I want you to wear."

"Arnez, I don't feel like going. You can go to the party. I'll wait in the hotel room for you."

If it wasn't for the severe stinging on my cheek I would've completely missed the smack that Arnez landed on my face. That's how sudden and unexpected it was to me.

"Don't you ever tell me what you won't do. Do you not know who I am? But don't worry, you'll learn. As I said, you have soldier potential. Nobody has taken the time to teach you but I will."

"You hit me...I can't believe you hit me." I really couldn't. Too many things didn't fuck me up in terms of disbelief but this had. I didn't think Arnez was a softie but woman beater went right over my head. He was passionate but gentle as a lover. The few times we went out he was a complete gentleman. He was not the man I would pick out of a line up to be the type who would snatch-a-ho-up on some bullshit but he was that man. After he slapped me, I stared in his eyes and saw that he was crazier than me and that was scary.

"Believe it. It's part of training camp. If you're a fast learner I'll only have to do it a few more times. But you're very young so you might be hard headed which means I'll have to knock you around several times before I break you in."

That fool said that shit like he was about to train me and put me through something simple like a cooking course. I could tolerate a bunch of bullshit from a nigga I was feeling. I even got off on some excitement in a relationship but a motherfucker beating my ass never turned me on. Because a nigga that would beat your ass is a nigga that would kill you and the bottom line was I didn't want to die. Now instead of focusing my energy on how to one-up Precious, I had to figure how to get the fuck away from Arnez's crazy ass.

"I'm a fast learner. You won't have any more problems from me. If you want me to go to the party then I will."

"That's my girl. Now go shower and get dressed. Like I said, we need to leave."

On the ride to New York, I was plotting on how I would break free of Arnez. Luckily I was born and raised there so I knew how to maneuver my way around with no problem. But I had to be careful. I already had Precious aiming at me, I didn't need to add a psycho like Arnez to the list.

"Turn the music down, this is an important call." I was about to ask him what was wrong with his hands but quickly remembered who I was dealing with and a remark like that might land me a blackened eye.

"You've been hard to catch up with the last couple of days."

"My wife got back home so I've been extremely busy." *Oh shit, that sounds like Supreme!* Now I was happy as hell I turned the volume down because their conversation was clear as shit.

"I understand, family always comes first." I had to roll my eyes hearing that come out of Arnez's mouth. He seemed like the type that would have his entire family petrified that if everything wasn't precisely the way he wanted everybody was getting fucked up.

"Yeah, but what's up with you. I thought for sure

you would have that Nico situation resolved by now."

"Me too but for the last few months he hasn't been making any moves…no business. Something had him occupied."

"Or someone."

"Excuse me?"

"Nothing, so what's up with him now?'

"Word came to me today that he might be partnering up with a woman named CoCo and this dude Genesis."

"Who the fuck are they?"

"Some people I'm not on good terms with. So if he's dealing with them, I would need to come up with a different approach in getting him to do some business with me."

"I advise you to come up with that approach at rapid speed because I've funneled way too much money in your business for you to bring me nothing."

"You know that I appreciate all that you've done."

"I don't need your appreciation or want it. If you can't get done what I need you to do then I'll have to take my money someplace else."

"Come on, we've worked together way too long for you to say something like that. I've made you millions of dollars."

"Yeah whatever."

"I got you. When you asked me to resolve that issue I didn't think it would be that complicated. But you know the problems I've had recently and like I said he's just starting to get back to handling business. There's a delay, that's all. But not the sort of problem that you would need to sever our business relationship."

"I hear you. I have to come that way tomorrow to stop by my parents' place to pick up my daughter, so before I leave I wanna see you. And our conversation needs to go differently. You know what you need to get done...so make it happen. I want Nico Carter out of commission...'nough said."

I had been dissecting each sentence from that discussion and I couldn't figure all the shit out but one thing seemed evident, Arnez worked for Supreme and Arnez was a drug dealer. So added to Supreme's list of business ventures was running a drug empire. I didn't think Xavier Mills had it in him. Now I had another reason why it was imperative I get the fuck away from Arnez. Because Supreme was coming to town and if he found out Arnez was dealing with me, I would be added to that out of commission list Nico Carter was on.

"I have to get rid of Genesis and CoCo once and for all. They're going to fuck everything up." I heard Arnez mumbling under his breath. I hoped if I remained mute he would continue on oblivious I was interested in every word he was saying.

"If I could just find Genevieve because having someone make prank calls pretending to be his sister isn't enough. I need her for bait."

Damn this nigga off the chain, getting fake motherfuckers to call pretending to be that man's sister. If he wasn't a woman beater, we could put our minds together and come up with some fabulous scams. He's more calculating than me.

"We're going to the Greenhouse in Soho. 150 Varick Street between Vandam & Spring," Arnez told the taxi driver. After letting him know our destination he turned his attention to me. "Did I tell you how sexy you look in that dress?"

"No, but you have great taste in clothes, so it's all you."

"True, but you've pulled if off perfectly," he said, admiring the black Alexander Wang sheer sleeved mini-dress. It was a cute dress, I'll admit. But Arnez had me feeling like I was his personal dress up doll which wasn't cute.

"So who is this party for?"

"The spokes model for Akil Walker's new women's clothing line."

"Oh, I've seen a couple of ads for that, his shit is hot. So he's giving the party for the person who's modeling his clothes?"

"She's the exclusive model for his women's line. And this is like her introduction to the heavyweights in the industry."

"Sounds exciting for her."

"I'm sure it will be." Arnez didn't strike me as the type who would give a fuck about some models' party to celebrate her introduction to the scene. I knew there was a lot more to this but I would have to sit back and observe to find out.

When the taxi pulled in front of the club it had that red velvet rope, I wanna be a star feel. Two cut the fuck up security men were keeping post at the entrance and some chick with a clipboard and headpiece was working the guest list. Arnez said a couple of words to the girl and slid on through. The spacious bi-level club was cute in a unique sort of way. I noticed a little sign that read 'first eco-friendly nightlife destination' I assumed that was important to the folks running the establishment because me as a guest could care less.

I followed behind Arnez taking in the interesting design of the place. The transparent ceiling fixture had a bunch of crystals, which seemed to be designed to emulate a rolling landscape. Then the bars were clear glass, that displayed lush natural scenes and I assumed it was all recycled since this was supposed to be an eco-friendly spot. None of it was my style but when I noticed the interior projection screens mounted on three separate walls playing what seemed to be the photo shoots the spokes model did for the clothing line. Then the name 'Nichelle' kept flashing on the screen and I assumed that was the model's name.

"Come on, we're going to sit in the VIP section on the upper level." I nodded my head and kept following Arnez, curious as to what he was up to.

"Maya," I heard someone call out my name but Soho

wasn't my neck of the woods so I glanced around to see who it might be. "Maya…" I heard the same female voice again. But this time I saw who it was.

"Tashawn, girl what are you doing here?" We gave each other a quick hug.

"You remember Dionne."

"Yeah, you talking 'bout Dionne from Queens?"

"Exactly, she dragged me to this bullshit. She heard Akil Walker would be here and thought if she showed up, she'd get discovered and be his next spokes model." We both burst out laughing because that sounded like some dreamer shit Dionne would come up with.

"Has she found him?"

"Hell no! And if she did, his head is probably so far up the ass of his new model up there," Tashawn pointed toward the projection screen, "so he wouldn't give Dionne a second thought. Plus she know the PR chick that put this shit together and supposedly Akil nor is that model Nichelle showing up. Akil's publicity people just threw that out there to get a bigger turn out and I see it worked…but moving on, what are you doing here. We ain't seen you in none of the boroughs for a minute. Where you been?"

"I've been in Miami for a minute."

"So what brought you here?"

"Him," I said pointing at Arnez who was making gestures for me to bring my ass on.

"Girl, he don't look cool wit' you being over here talking to me."

"That nigga a nut. Don't nothing make him happy but himself. You driving?"

"Yeah, why?"

"How much longer you gon' be here?"

"Dionne in the bathroom. When she come out we probably leaving in a few. This not my type of party. And Dionne only came to meet that Akil dude, now that she know he ain't showing up, she ready to go."

"I hear that so can you do me a favor?"

"Sure, what is it?"

"Let me get a ride wit' ya'."

"Girl, that ain't nothing. It'll be like old times when we used to skip school together and ride the trains going no fuckin' where."

"Yeah, but we ain't getting on the train…not tonight," we laughed thinking about old times.

"So do you want me to just come get you when we're ready?"

"I'ma ditch homeboy so I don't want him to have a clue I'm bouncing. Here put my number in your phone. I'll meet you on the corner of Spring within ten minutes. But if I don't show up, you got my number, send me a text."

"Cool, we'll be in a black Explorer."

"Thanks, Tashawn. Girl, I owe you big time." I was so happy I ran into Tashawn, I was tempted to break into a two-step in the middle of the dance floor. But I remained cool and smiled when I reached Arnez. He appeared as if he was ready to choke a bitch up.

"Who were you talking to?"

"This girl I went to school with. I hadn't seen her in a minute so we were playing catch up. So what's up, are you enjoying the party?" I asked wanting to switch the dialogue off of me.

"It's cool, I just wish the guest of honor would hurry up, show her face."

"You talking about her, that model Nichelle?" I pointed at the screen.

"Yes, but her name is Genevieve," he huffed like I didn't know who I was talking about.

"Huh? That model up there, her name is Nichelle."

"Yes her…"he shrugged, seeming annoyed.

"Oh baby, that's the closest you gon' get to seeing her face."

"What are you talking about?'

"She's a no-show and so is the dude Akil."

"Who told you that?" he practically screamed the question in my ear.

"There's no need to get upset. I'm sure you'll be able to see them at some other party."

"Just answer the question," he pulled on my arm.

"Listen, I'm getting tired of you manhandling me!" I was ready to take off my shoe and go upside dude's head but since I knew I was about to make a getaway I calmed it down. "I apologize baby, what was the question again?"

"How do you know Genevieve isn't showing up?"

"Who is this Genevieve chick you keep talking

about?"

"Excuse me, I meant to say Nichelle."

"The girl I was speaking with, her girlfriend is cool with the PR chick that did this event and she told her neither one of them was showing up."

"Are you sure?"

"I mean I wasn't there taking part in the discussion but I'm sure you can go ask the girl yourself. My friend told me she was upstairs. Ask for the PR chick and she's wearing one of those headsets."

"You stay right here." Arnez pointed his finger in my face like I was five years old. "I'll be right back."

"No problem baby, take your time I'll be right here...Not!" When I saw Arnez motherfuckin' ass make that turn to go upstairs I grabbed my purse and hit it. Whatever shit he had bought me at the mall he could keep it. I had all the essential goods right here in my purse. I bolted out that club so fast and never looked back.

Precious

I stood in Aaliyah's bedroom thinking about all I had missed out on from being away from her these past few months. Looking at her pictures, she had grown so much. Although she looked a lot like me, it was amazing how much she resembled my mother. When I came across one particular picture on her dresser, it took every ounce of strength I had not to completely lose it.

"Yo' ass will be mine! I don't give a fuck what I have to do!" I spit, holding a picture that Maya and Aaliyah took together. The anger that had come over me wanted to rip the picture into tiny shreds, but then I was torn, because my sweet Aaliyah was also in the picture, and for some strange reason I would feel guilty tearing up her image too. So, I did the only other thing I felt comfortable with. I tossed the shit in the trash.

"We're gonna take a flight out in the morning."

I jolted slightly, not expecting to hear Supreme's voice.

"I didn't mean to startle you."

"That's okay. What time does our flight leave?"

"We're taking the jet, so whenever we get there."

"Well, I'll be ready first thing in the morning, because I can't wait to see my baby."

"I know she'll be happy to see you too."

"Do you really think so? I mean it's been so long that I'm afraid she won't remember me."

"Of course Aaliyah remembers you. I always showed her your picture and told her that this was her mommy."

"You did?" The shock in my voice was evident.

"Yeah, I did. I know, as angry as I was with you, it surprised me too, but something just made me do it. And I'm glad I did."

"So am I. I know with everything you believed, the last person you wanted to talk to Aaliyah about was me."

"For the last couple of days I've been tearing this house up, searching for that necklace."

"I was wondering what you were looking for."

"In my heart I knew what you told me was true, but…"

"You weren't totally convinced," I said, completing Supreme's thought. "I knew that. That's why you still haven't touched me, because part of you believes that all this time I've been having this fling with Nico, that I left you and Aaliyah to be with him. I do pray that you find that necklace so you can put your mind at ease and have some sort of proof that I'm telling you the truth."

"I know that you are," Supreme disclosed as he moved his arm from behind his back and lifted up the necklace. "It was in a satin pouch in the pocket of a coat hanging in a closet I never knew existed. That's what happens when you live in a house that's way too big."

"Baby, I'm so happy you found it," I sighed, feeling for the first time that there was a chance Supreme and I could get back what we once had.

"If you want, I can put it back on for you."

"Of course I want you to." I walked to the hallway where Supreme was standing and turned around. He lifted my hair and latched the necklace around my neck, putting it back in its rightful place. I then felt the softness of his lips on my shoulder, and he began sprinkling kisses up to my neck. A warm shiver shot through my body as it yearned for the touch of my husband.

"Damn, I missed you!" Supreme whispered in my ear before the tip of his tongue stroked my earlobe. He turned me around and pressed my back against the wall, sliding his hand up the loose fitting dress I was wearing. The firm pressure from his hand caressed the flesh of my thigh.

"Baby, I missed you more," I said breathlessly.

My arms were pinned up and my eyes were closed as I gave in to the pleasure I'd been longing for. Supreme's tongue made love to every inch of my body before he even entered inside me. When he lifted his shirt off, the flexing of each muscle reminded me of how secure I felt in his arms. I needed him so badly that it scared me. He clasped his hands around my waist and lifted me up, and then laid me down in the middle of the hallway. I didn't mind, because I couldn't wait any longer and the bedroom seemed too far away. I wrapped my legs around his back and pulled him in closer as our kisses became more intense and our tongues went deeper. Then, when he let his long thick dick massage my clit, I had an orgasm based on the anticipation alone. And once he dipped inside of me, if possible, I fell in love with him all over again. It was clear that emotionally, physically and mentally, we were both trying to make up for all the months of being apart, which made our lovemaking that much more passionate, and let me know that I was finally home.

When the private jet landed at Teterboro Airport, I was anxious to go to Supreme's parents' house and get Aaliyah. I missed my baby so much that it hurt.

"Listen, I have some business I need to handle. The car will take you to my parents' house, and I'll be there later on when I'm done."

"I don't want to be away from you. Can we go get Aaliyah and then we come with you?"

"Precious, this is business, not pleasure. I'll be back

as soon as I can," Supreme promised, kissing my hand.

"Okay, baby." I watched as he got into the other awaiting limousine. I speculated about what business was so important that he had to go directly from the jet to handle. But I also understood that the lifestyle we lived required more money than I ever thought was possible to even make. Maintaining this standard of living required a lot of work from Supreme. So, if he had to go and handle business, then I had no choice but to understand no matter how much I wanted to spend time with him.

After Supreme's limo drove off, I got into the other one. Before I could even get comfortable, my cell started ringing and saw it was Nico calling. "Hey you!"

"Hey you back. I hadn't heard from you since your flight landed and wanted to make sure you were straight."

"Everything's good. I actually just got to New Jersey."

"Jersey, what you doing there?"

"Supreme and I came to pick up Aaliyah. She was here visiting his parents."

"Well, let me let you go, 'cause I know he doesn't want you talking to me."

"I'm alone. He had to go handle some business, so he's gonna meet up with us later."

"Cool. I know you can't wait to see your daughter."

"Nico, with all the bullshit I've been through these last few months, holding Aaliyah again will make it all worthwhile. But I'm still gonna stick it to Maya's ass. Speaking of Maya, have you gotten any new leads?"

"I was gonna wait until I got more facts before

telling you, but since you brought her name up—"

"Tell me!" I insisted, cutting Nico off.

"Maya might be in New York. One of the investigators on the case said they believe she was spotted in her old neighborhood. He's had someone watching her mother's house for some time, but hadn't seen any activity. But supposedly yesterday she was seen in the area. This hasn't been verified yet, so I don't want you getting amped just yet."

"So, when do you think you'll know for sure?"

"I can't say; maybe in the next few hours, maybe not until tomorrow. But of course I'll call you the moment I get the facts."

"Are you still in Philly?"

"Yeah, but me and Genesis are heading that way now."

"You and Genesis?'

"Yeah. I told him I wanted to already be in New York in case what the investigator told me turned out to be accurate. He said he had some business to handle that way, so he would take the ride with me."

"I really do appreciate you staying on top of this for me. With everything I got going on, I don't want Maya to slip through the cracks."

"And she won't! You need time to reconnect with your family, so I'ma hold this shit down for you...no worries."

"I gotta feeling Maya might really be in New York. She knows I'm with Supreme, so she can't go back to

Miami, and—"

"Hold up! Maya knows you're back with Supreme?"

"I've been so occupied tryna' get shit right with my husband that I forgot to tell you. I spoke to her."

"When?"

"The other day. She called Supreme and I answered. At first she was on some juvenile bullshit, playing on the phone. You know, hanging up then calling back. Finally, I called her ass out and she spoke up."

"What did she say?"

"Nothing much. She basically listened. I told her ass to enjoy her little freedom, because I was gon' tap that ass when I saw her. She tried to act like she wasn't shook, but I could tell I had the hussy nervous."

"I bet."

"That's why I believe she probably is in New York. She knows she can't come back to Supreme. With Devon dead, there's no need for her to stay in Philly, so why not go back to her comfort zone in New York to come up with a master plan?"

"True…but before you even told me about your conversation with Maya, I felt the same way. That's why I decided to head to New York. But now, with what you just told me, basically confirms it."

"Well, we're pulling up to Supreme's parents' house. Call me when you get to New York or find out anything else…whichever comes first."

"Got you. And I know she's never met me, but please give Aaliyah a hug and kiss for me."

"That's so sweet, and I will. Bye."

I couldn't get out of the limo fast enough. By the time the driver got out to open my door, I was about to ring the bell. Mr. Mills must've heard the limo pull up, because he came out with open arms before I reached the entrance.

"It's wonderful to see you, Precious!" He said, giving me a hug.

"It's great to see you too. Where's Aaliyah?"

"With Grandma," Mr. Mills said affectionately. "They went to the park earlier, and they're on their way back now. I know how excited you must be."

"I am. I miss her like crazy."

"She misses you too. We told her yesterday that Mommy was coming to get her, and she's been smiling ever since."

I followed Mr. Mills inside the house, anxious for my baby to come home. "I see Aaliyah has her toys everywhere," I commented, looking around.

"Yeah, that's one of the beautiful things about having grandchildren. They're so full of life. With their toys and curiosity, they can't help but keep us old folks full of life too."

"I know you all were planning on having Aaliyah much longer, and I apologize for cutting her visit so short, but…"

"You don't have to apologize for wanting your child to go home with you. I know that you, Supreme and the baby have been through hell. I'm just pleased you all have come back together and are trying to work things out."

"I am too."

"We've been married for over thirty-five years, and it hasn't been easy. I know it's hard work, but my son loves you, and I can look into your eyes and see that you love him a hell of a lot too."

"I do...I really, really do. I just hope our marriage can last as long as you and Mrs. Mills' has."

"Stay faithful and in prayer, and it will...hold on, let me answer the phone. Have a seat and get comfortable. They'll be home soon," Mr. Mills continued before leaving the room.

A big smile crossed my face, and I sat down on the couch with an enormous amount of happiness consuming every part of me. For months, I didn't think I would ever feel this sort of contentment again. But here I was, sitting in the living room of my husband's parents' house, waiting for the arrival of my daughter. Growing up, I never experienced this sort of normalcy, and I had to admit, it was one of the most gratifying feelings in the world. My daydreaming of feeling on top of the world was interrupted when Mr. Mills came back into the living room.

"Mr. Mills, what's wrong?" His once jovial face now appeared to be cracked and broken.

"We have to go to the hospital."

"What happened?" I jumped up. "Say something!"

"My wife has a minor concussion, and Aaliyah's gone." Mr. Mills' voice was calm, but his hands were shaking and fear consumed his face.

"What do you mean Aaliyah is gone?"

"I don't know what happened yet. The police officer didn't know all the details."

"The police! Oh Dear God, this can't be happening to me, not again! Let's go, now!" I screamed, rushing out of the house.

When we got to Mrs. Mills' hospital room, she was sitting up in the bed and incoherent. Tears welled up in her eyes when she saw my face.

"Precious, I'm so sorry! I'll never forgive myself if anything happens to Aaliyah!" Tears were now streaming down her face, and I swear to you, I honestly didn't care. Her tears meant nothing to me.

"It's okay," Mr. Mills said, trying to console his wife.

"No, it's not okay! What happened to my daughter?"

"After we were finished playing at the park, we walked to the car, and when I was buckling her in the car seat, somebody snuck up behind me and knocked me on the back of my head. I must've loss consciousness, because when I woke up I was in the hospital bed."

"Thank God you're alright!" Mr. Mills said, rubbing his wife's shoulders. "It wasn't your fault," he continued, and then he turned to look at me, wanting confirmation that I didn't blame Mrs. Mills. He was right, it wasn't her fault, but it didn't change how fucked up I felt at this very moment.

"Are you the missing little girl's mother?" a police officer entered the room and asked.

"Yes I am, but can you wait one moment? I need to take this call." I sprinted out the room, wanting some privacy.

"Nico, somebody took Aaliyah, and I put it on everything that Maya's motherfuckin' ass had something to do with it!"

"Get the fuck outta here! When did this happen?"

"It couldn't have been no more than an hour or so ago. She was at the park with Supreme's mother, and somebody rolled up on her from behind and knocked her out. Then, they took Aaliyah. That sounds like a Maya move."

"Fuckin' right! She's desperate. She knows you're holding all the cards, so what can she do but revert back to the only thing that gives her leverage...Aaliyah! I might have to kill that bitch myself!" Nico roared. "Wait, hold on one second, that's the P.I. beeping in on the other line."

I wanted to leap out of my skin as I paced the hospital floor. Fuckin' around with Maya's demented ass was gon' have me with a head full of gray hair before I even knocked on thirty.

"He got something!" Were the first words Nico said when he clicked back over.

"What did he say?"

"Early this morning, Maya rented a car over at Enterprise."

"Which one?"

"The one in Englewood."

"She must've stopped there before she took Aaliyah, because Supreme's parents live in Teaneck which isn't far from Englewood at all."

"Yeah, because the dude that helped her said she didn't have a baby with her. But she did ask him if he could recommend a hotel in the area, and he suggested the Crown Plaza on South Van Brunt Street. She even asked him for directions and he wrote them down for her."

"I'm on my way over there."

"Precious, why don't you wait for me? We just passed Exit 13 on the turnpike."

"I'll see you there. I gotta go get my daughter!" I rushed back to Mrs. Mills' hospital room on a mission.

"Mr. Mills, I need your car keys."

"Why, you're leaving? You should stay here. Supreme is on his way."

"I'll call Supreme when I get in the car, but I need your car keys, now!" Mr. Mills just stood there staring at me like he didn't hear what the fuck I said. "Am I speaking a foreign language? I need your car keys, now!"

"Give her the keys." Mrs. Mills smacked her husband's arm, and he reluctantly handed over the keys to me.

"Thanks!" I said, snatching them out of his hand and rushing out. I heard the officer calling out, trying to get my attention, but I ignored him, because for what I was about to do, the police would only be in the way. I know I had agreed with Nico that our first option was to let the legal system work and let Maya rot in jail, but that option was now off the table. Maya was now officially a dead bitch!

Maya

"This baby is so cute! Whose little girl is this?" Tashawn asked me while she looked at a sleeping Aaliyah.

"She's my niece."

"I didn't know Mike had a baby."

"Yeah, he found out about her while he was locked up. And before he got killed, he always told me that if anything happened to him to make sure I took care of her."

"She is such a cutie. She do kinda look like him."

"I think so too."

"So, where's the little girl's mom at?"

"She fell on hard times and she ain't really got no family. She called me yesterday asking if I could keep her for awhile, you know, until she got back on her feet.

That's my niece so I couldn't say no."

"True. That's real big of you though, Maya. Kids ain't no joke. They're a big responsibility. My sister got one, and she stays struggling."

"Exactly. I'm just glad I was in New York, which made it easy for me to go pick Aaliyah up from her."

"Yeah, that worked out good. So, how long are you staying? I mean, a hotel ain't exactly the best place for a baby."

"I know, and I need to get her so much stuff. I mean homegirl didn't even give me no clothes or nothing."

"Damn, she must've fell on real hard times. But I guess she was doing the best she could, because the baby looks like she was well cared for."

"Yeah, but I need to get her some stuff before we hit the road. That's why I asked you to meet me here. I was hoping you could watch Aaliyah while I went to the store and got some stuff for her."

"Oh, you need me to baby-sit? Girl, that ain't no problem, and she's asleep."

"Tashawn, you my girl. This is the second time you've come through for me. Here, take this," I said, going in my wallet and pulling out some money.

"This is five hundred dollars! What you want, for me to babysit her for the month!"

"Tashawn, you so silly!"

"You don't have to give me all this money."

"What, you don't want it?" I said, reaching out my hand.

"I ain't say all that," she laughed, tightly gripping the money and pulling her hand back. "I ain't crazy. If you want me to have it, I won't turn it down. I was just sayin' it wasn't necessary to give me this much."

"Girl, don't worry about it. I appreciate you helping me out at the last minute like this. I shouldn't be gone that long, because I really want to hit the road tonight."

"Where you going?"

"We have to stop through Philly for a minute before we go to our new home."

"You bought a house?"

"Yep, it's in Miami, and it's beautiful."

"Damn girl, you doing good for yourself. Your money must be right—or should I say *his* money!"

"No, it's all mine. Mike had a huge insurance policy, and when he died all the money came to me."

"He didn't leave none for his daughter?"

"Well, he wasn't sure how stable her mother was, and he didn't want her to splurge all the money on herself and then his baby end up with nothing anyway. He knew I would make sure that if need be, my niece would be taken care of."

"You proved him right. Well, girl, when ya' get situated, you need to let me come visit you in Miami. I ain't never been there before, and I heard it's the shit!"

"Yeah, you'll love it. I'll definitely send for you so we can ball out and pop some bottles and shit."

"That's what's up!"

"Girl, let me head out and handle my shit before

Aaliyah wakes up."

"Take your time. I know how to care for a baby. I baby-sit my nephew all the time. I got this."

"Thanks, girl. Hit me on my cell if you need anything."

"Will do."

As I rode the elevator down, I thought about how perfectly shit was coming together for me. Overhearing the conversation between Supreme and Arnez while we were in the car made the bullshit I had to deal with from that maniac Arnez worth it. I would've never known Aaliyah was with Supreme's parents, and my window of opportunity to snatch her up was a small one. I had to move swiftly if I wanted to get the job done.

From the months of living with Supreme and Aaliyah visiting his parents during that time, I knew their address, which was a serious plus point. After I had a cab drop me off at the rental car place not far from their house, and once I got the vehicle, all I had to do was park in an inconspicuous place and wait for the right opening to make my move. When I saw Supreme's mother come out of the house with Aaliyah, I knew the opportunity had come knocking. Once I followed them to the park and let grandma wear her little granddaughter's ass out, it was too easy to knock the defenseless old lady to the ground and take Aaliyah.

Now that I had the best bargaining tool possible, when the time was right, I would contact Supreme and see exactly what he was willing to give up to get his daughter back, or *who* he was willing to give up, because I refused to allow Precious to be happy. She thought she could come back and reclaim her old life as if shit hadn't changed. The nerve of her answering Supreme's phone as if she owned him. But once again, I showed her who the real queen bitch is, and it's me. I'm always one step ahead of her.

I would've given anything to see the look on her face when she got the news that the reunion with her daughter she'd been wishing for was not gonna happen. I couldn't help but laugh to myself. Precious had come up short once again. For a second time, I was the hand rocking the cradle, so that means I rule the world.

Skipping to the car, smiles and giggles continued as I thought about all the misery I was bringing Precious. *That bitch is somewhere crying right now, and Supreme probably so sick of all the drama that comes with dealing with her ass that he ain't thinking about wiping away the tears. Yep, Precious, when I'm done torturing you, you will have lost it all; your daughter, husband and mind.*

"Oh shi-i-i-i-t!" I bawled as my moment of celebrating was instantly brought to a halt. Right as I put the key in the ignition, I saw Precious in some sort of old school Cadillac, cruising slowly as she looked around the parking lot. There was no doubt in my mind she was looking for me. When the car started, the sound of the engine must've caught her attention, and the evil glare she hurled in my direction made me put the car quickly in reverse and then into drive, and I sped the fuck out of the parking lot. Of course her nerve-wrecking ass was on my shit as I hit South Van Brunt going towards Nordhoff Place. I then suddenly veered to the right on Route-4W hoping to lose the bitch, but when I looked in the rearview mirror, there she was, keeping the fuck up. I then made another abrupt right, which put me on Decatur, and that insistent broad did too.

"Bitch, get off my back!" I screamed out, determined to lose her once and for all. When I tried to make a hasty left on Alfred Avenue, I lost control of the car and smashed into a parked car. The impact was so hard that it caused the airbag to discharge.

"Fu-u-u-u-uck!" I shouted as I tried to start the car back up, but got absolutely nothing. "Fuck it…fuck it… fuck it!" I repeated as I grabbed my purse and soared out of the car, concluding that I would have to lose this bitch on foot.

I glanced behind me briefly and didn't see Precious, which brought a small sense of relief. I cut through some houses trying to maneuver through the back streets.

"Damn, I'm tired," I groaned, almost out of breath. I knew I couldn't run forever, so I decided to call Tashawn. It was either call her, or a taxi, and I was too tired, frustrated and pissed the fuck off to try and get some local taxi information.

"Hello."

"Hey Tashawn," I said, still breathing extremely hard.

"Maya, are you okay? You sound out of breath."

"Girl, somebody just tried to rob me."

"What!"

"Yes, I was able to keep my purse, but they took the car."

"Are you serious? Did you call the police?"

"Yes, I'm waiting for them now so I can file a report. But can you pick me up? I could ask the police officer when he gets here, but I need to go back to the rental car place, and I know that they're not gonna want to do all that for me."

"Don't even trip. I'm sure you don't wanna ride in no police car anyway. Tell me where you at and I'll come get you."

"What about my niece?"

"Girl, I have a car seat. I always keep one in the car because I never know when I might have to go get my nephew."

"Great, I owe you again."

"You gave me five-hundred dollars, so we good. Now where you at?"

"There's this gas station right beside this store on the corner of Hancock Avenue. You know, like if you were going towards Route-4 E."

"I think I know where you talking about, but I got navigation on my phone so I'll be straight."

"Girl, you really are a life saver."

"Don't worry about it. I'll call you when I get near there."

"Cool, I'll be there." I stood behind a house for a few

more minutes. I could see a main street, and a gas station right next to a store, from where I was. After making sure there was no sign of Precious, I felt confident enough to walk across the street and wait for Tashawn near the gas station. When I went to the store, I was thirsty and I had to piss, so I figured I'd empty my bladder first, then get a drink.

I dashed inside the stall, almost ripping off my jeans. I didn't even have time to lock the door because I was afraid I was about to urinate on myself. When I bent down over the toilet, I shut my eyes in relief as the pee seemed to flow forever. When I finished, I felt much more relaxed. My mind was now clear enough to figure out my next move. "At least I got rid of Precious' dumb ass," I said, after flushing the toilet.

"Think again, bitch!"

My heart dropped when I realized Precious was standing in front of the bathroom stall with her fists balled up, each resting solidly on her waist. Before I could say a word, her spiked stiletto heel was puncturing my stomach, thrusting me back against the mechanical flush valve.

"Ahhhhhhh!" I screeched out in pain. I thought I heard my back crack, but before I had time to know for sure, Precious was digging her nails in my scalp as she slammed my head inside the toilet bowl.

"You just had to keep fuckin' wit' me and my family!" she yelled, yanking my head out of the toilet bowl water. "You gon' regret the day you ever decided to go up against me!" she continued, then jammed my face back in the water. This heffa had me thinking I was gonna drown in the toilet bowl. I was trying to clench my hands on the floor to get some balance and maybe get Precious off of me, but she was not letting up.

Precious yanked my head out of the toilet again, and I tried to catch my breath thinking she was gonna baptize me once more, but instead, as she maintained the grip on my hair, she opened the stall door and slammed me against the wall.

"I want you to see my face as I beat yo' ass! Oh, and check out the pink diamond heart. Yeah, bitch this shit is where it belongs." Precious barked before taking her knee and shoving it up my pussy, not once, not twice, not even three fuckin' times, but over and over again. I felt like the bitch was giving me a botched abortion, and I wasn't even pregnant.

"I can't take no more…please, stop!" I begged.

"Stop! Bitch, we ain't even started!" she boasted, smashing the back of my head repeatedly against the wall. "You ain't so bad when you ain't got Devon holding me while you beat me wit' some brass knuckles, huh? Don't go silent on me. The fun just about to start."

My body was halfway numb from pain by the time Precious hauled me over to the sink. When she swung my face like it was a baseball bat against the bathroom faucets, I just knew I was dead. Blood splattered everywhere as my nose and mouth ripped open. The collision with the sink also caused my two front teeth to come out. Although I wasn't dead, I no longer wanted to be alive.

"Precious, you win...please stop!" I pleaded as blood gushed out of my mouth.

"I'ma be honest with you. I am gonna kill you. But if you take me to my daughter and not a strand of her hair is out of place, instead of mutilating you while you're still alive, I'll simply slit your throat and let you watch yourself bleed to death. You can decide while I'm taking you to the car.

Precious pushed me down on the floor, wrapped my hair around her hand and dragged me out of the bathroom as if I was a bloody ragdoll. I could see the horror and disbelief on some of the customers' faces who were in the store, but she didn't give a fuck about any of them. She kept pulling me down the aisle like this was her world. When she opened the door and I hit the pavement, it felt as if the concrete was ripping the skin from my face.

"Help me!" I called out barely audible because of the excruciating pain I was in, but it was as if nobody cared, or maybe they were too damn scared, because only a crazy motherfucker like Precious could be this bold. When we got to her car and she was opening the passenger side door, I heard a car zoom up and stop right in front of us. The way Precious had me positioned on the ground I couldn't see shit though.

"Yo, Precious! What the fuck are you doing!" I heard a male voice yell out.

"Before I murder this bitch, Maya is gonna take me

to my daughter…ain't that right, Maya?" Precious smiled down at me, knowing I didn't have the strength to reply even if I wanted to.

"I know you're pissed, but this shit right here is crazy. You're dragging a badly beaten woman out in public. I know how angry you are; fuck, I'm angry too, but this ain't the way to get shit done."

As I listened to some man trying to reason with Precious, I heard a car door open and then shut.

"Genesis, can you please try and reason with her?"

I felt Precious shift forward in one swift movement as if reaching for something, because of course, with the hold she had on my hair, when she moved, I moved too.

"Nico, get the fuck away from me! When I spotted Maya's sneaky ass crossing the street, I shoulda' never called you and told you where I was, 'cause I don't' want to hear this shit!"

"Yo, I can't believe you took my gun like that! Give me that shit back!" Precious stepped forward, evidently steadily holding the heat.

"Don't make me use this on you, because I will."

"Precious, what are you doing? you're smarter than this."

"Genesis, you need to stay the fuck outta this! You have no idea the hell this bitch has put me and my family through. And when I finally made it back to them, she kidnaps my daughter…again! This sick bitch deserves to die. Now, both of ya' get the fuck out of my way. I'm sure somebody is gon' call the police soon, if they haven't already. So I need to go!"

"Precious, Nico explained to me everything that Maya has done to you and your family, and she deserves to be punished. But I can't let you kill her."

"Excuse me? I didn't know I asked for your permission."

"Listen. I was trying to wait for Quentin to get here, but—"

"Quentin! What the fuck did you call Quentin for? Quentin ain't got nothing to do wit' this shit! Yo, get the fuck out of my way, both of you, before I just start blasting!"

"Precious, that's your sister you're about to kill, and Quentin Jacobs is both of ya's father. I swear it's true. When he saw you at that funeral and you told him your last name—not Mills but Cummings, unlike the first time when he met you with Mike—he had a feeling, but to be positive, when I had you meet me for breakfast that morning, it was to get your DNA so Quentin could have it compared to his."

"So what? You're a forensic scientist now? I can catch you on an episode of *CSI!* Nigga, get the fuck outta here with that bullshit!"

"It ain't bullshit, Precious. Maya is your sister."

"Let's say for argument sake you are telling the truth...so fuckin' what! I wouldn't give a damn if she came out my own mother's pussy and we were full blood sisters! This ho gotta go!"

"I'm not gonna let you spend the rest of your life in

jail because of Maya. You have a fuckin' daughter to live for! You've always been so hard headed and stubborn. Is this piece of shit really worth your life without your daughter in it? Especially since we got the proof we need to send her to jail. I've already been in contact with Detective Moore. He's hungry to lock her ass up, and I told him I have the evidence he needs to do it," Nico continued to try and plead his case.

I wasn't sure what distressed me more; learning that I had a father I knew nothing about, or a sister I despised. Either way, my life was completely fucked, or over. Because, if Precious spared my life, I would still spend the majority of it locked up in a cage, or she could kill me, and honestly at this point, that sounded like a better alternative.

"Precious, Nico is right. You have everything to live for and nothing to gain if you kill Maya. Give Nico the gun so we can go find your daughter. Isn't that what it's really about, being reunited with your daughter? Don't let your emotions cause you to make a bad decision that you'll have to pay the consequences for, for the rest of your life."

Whoever the nigga, Genesis was, he had a profound effect on Precious, because she did hand the gun over to Nico, and right then, I heard what sounded like an explosion.

"What the fuck!" Precious walked a few feet forward, still dragging my ass. I guess when she put the gun down, that didn't include putting me down too.

"Some truck and a car just crashed into each other.

I can't see how anybody could have survived that shit!"
Genesis said, as I assumed he had the best view of the
accident. "I'ma go check and see if anybody is alive and
needs some help."

"Precious, can I trust you won't go do no crazy shit
to Maya if I go see if I can be of any help to Genesis?"

"Nico, go head. I'm not gonna do nothing. You and
Genesis made your point. I'm positive Maya is gonna tell
me where my daughter is," she said, yanking my head.
"And then once we know Aaliyah's safe, we can toss
Maya's ass over to the police."

"A'ight, don't fuck around and do nothing stupid."

"I won't. Plus, Supreme should be here any minute
too. I had left him a message letting him know I spotted
Maya, and where I was at. See, I think that's him pulling
up now."

"Cool. I'ma check to see what's going on with the
accident, and I'll be back."

With the fucked up luck I had today, I would deal
with it all if it meant that Supreme wouldn't see me
like this. The idea that the last image of me inscribed
in Supreme's mind was of my cut up mouth and face,
missing teeth, and covered in blood, made me want to get
a hold of Nico's gun and end it all.

"What is Supreme doing? What is taking him so
long to come over here?" I heard Precious mumble to
herself out loud. "Genesis, did you see Supreme?"

"Yes."

"Where is he?"

"He's over there by the where the accident was."

"Oh, he's trying to help. That must mean there were some survivors."

"Precious, come with me for a minute."

"Hellooooo…Genesis…I have to stay here and watch Maya, remember."

"Here comes Nico. He'll make sure Maya doesn't go anywhere until the cops come arrest her. Nico, I was just telling Precious that you'll guard Maya while she comes with me."

"That's right. Go with Genesis. I got Maya."

"Ya' worry too much. I told you I wasn't gonna kill Maya. She still has to tell us where Aaliyah is. But if ya' feel better letting Nico play watchdog, then so be it. I wanna go talk to Supreme anyway."

When Precious unleashed my hair from her grasp, my head hit the pavement so hard that my once fading headache was back. I managed to lift my head up and caught a glimpse of lights flashing and sirens roaring from the ambulances that were on the scene. Precious was completely out of my view, and it was Nico who was now beside me.

"Thank you for not letting Precious kill me."

"Don't thank me yet," he said, pulling out his gun and sticking the barrel to my head. "Do you know who was in one of those cars that crashed? Aaliyah! And so help me, if she dies, I promise you, I will kill you myself."

After Nico's warning, a piercing scream filled the air, and I knew it was the cries from my sister…Precious.

Precious

"My baby can't die! Supreme, do something!" I screamed, becoming hysterical as we entered the emergency room.

"We're going to need you to wait here," the paramedics ordered as they rushed Aaliyah in.

"Precious, she'll pull through," Supreme said, trying to sound encouraging, but it wasn't working.

"This can't be happening. When will this hell we're living in end?" I wanted to know as my hands were shaking and my voice cracked.

"Your daughter doesn't have any medical conditions or allergies, correct?" the ER nurse asked.

"No, I already told the paramedics that on the ride over in the ambulance."

"I understand, sir. I was just checking, taking every

precaution."

"How is she?" Nico asked frantically, walking in with Genesis.

"What the fuck is he doing here?" Supreme barked, making it clear that Nico's presence was not wanted.

"Supreme, please! Nico is concerned, just like Genesis.

"Mr. and Mrs. Mills," we heard the doctor call out.

"Yes! How is our daughter? Is she going to be okay?"

"I'm Dr. Katz. We're going to do everything we can to save your daughter. She's being prepped for surgery as we speak."

"Are you saying she might die? Oh God, no!" My knees buckled underneath me, and I would've hit the floor if Supreme hadn't been there to hold me up.

"Excuse me, I have to go to your daughter," Dr. Katz told us, rushing off and leaving me in a state of shock.

"Precious, what did the doctor say?" Nico asked, coming near Supreme and I.

"She's about to go into surgery. My baby can't die... she just can't!" My voice sounded almost tranquil. I let go of Supreme's hand and went to sit down. I refused to believe that my daughter would die. If she did, then somebody should walk up to me right now and kill me too.

This was all too much. Nothing made any sense. Right when I was about to kill Maya, I learned that she is supposedly my sister, and that Quentin Carter might be our father. Then some chick who was on her way to pick Maya up gets in a horrible accident that kills her and leaves my daughter barely holding on to her life. Everything that could go wrong had, and now it seemed to be getting worse. This wasn't the happy ending I had envisioned. It was actually more horrible than anything I could've imagined.

"I know that feeling you have right now, but you have to fight against giving into it," I heard Genesis say as he placed his hand on my shoulder.

"How do you do that? Tell me, please, because it hurts more than anything I could've ever imagined."

"When Talisa died, I knew my son's chances of surviving were slim to none, but I stayed in prayer and kept the faith," Genesis divulged as he bent down in front of me and placed my hands in his. "You have to do the same. Aaliyah needs you to be strong, and so does your husband. Because trust me when I tell you, he may not admit it, but the pain he's in has him ready to take out this entire hospital if they don't save his daughter's life."

"Genesis, I've been strong all my life. I didn't have a choice, if only to avoid becoming a statistic. The life I was born into was one where being nothing was expected. When I married Supreme and had Aaliyah, she was supposed to have everything I was denied growing up: a loving father, beautiful home, and a mother who protected her. I got the first two right, but I've failed miserably with the last one."

"Precious, this isn't your fault. You had no control

over what Maya did, or that girl who was driving the car Aaliyah was in."

"Then why do I feel responsible?"

"Because you're a mother, and that's your child. It's called 'love' and it's the most powerful tool we have as parents. So, hold onto that love and use it to fight for Aaliyah. It's easy to give into the pain and feel defeated, but for the sake of your daughter and husband, don't do it."

As I soaked in Genesis' words of wisdom. We both jumped in shock due to the loud interruption, courtesy of Supreme and Nico. They were having a heated exchange, which had escalated to a shoving match, and then Supreme threw a punch that landed on Nico's upper right jaw, and Nico returned the favor.

"Would the two of you stop!" I belted, pissed the fuck off that they would behave like immature little boys on the playground in the middle of such a major crisis.

Before shit got any further out of hand, Genesis was able to break them apart. "Nico, chill. This ain't the time or place for this bullshit." Genesis pulled Nico away, taking him to the other side of the waiting area.

"Supreme, our daughter is in there fighting for her life, and you want to fight with Nico! What the hell is wrong with you?"

"He shouldn't be here! I'm sick and tired that every time I turn around this motherfucker wants to be up in your face."

"That's not what's going on right now. He was there

when the accident happened. Of course he's gonna want to make sure that Aaliyah is okay, just like Genesis. I understand the two of you don't like each other, but I don't need this shit right now, and neither does Aaliyah. She needs all of our prayers while she's in surgery fighting for her life."

"I know, baby. I'm sorry," Supreme said, embracing me tightly as I closed my eyes, giving in to the calmness of the moment. I felt so safe in his arms, as if he could protect me from anything.

That moment of calmness didn't last long, because when I opened my eyes I saw Quentin Jacobs walk in. I broke free from Supreme to confront him. "What the hell are you doing here? You need to leave, now!"

"Precious!" Genesis stated in a hardened tone as if he knew he was my voice of reason.

"I wanted to see how my daughter and granddaughter were doing."

When those words came out of Quentin's mouth, it made me want to vomit. "Why don't you go check on Maya? She's the only daughter that needs you!"

"You're also my daughter. You both need me."

"I can't take anymore of this *Maury Povich* bullshit! This is public property. If you want to stay in this hospital, so be it. But stay the hell away from me and my family."

"I'll respect your wishes, but here, please take this." Quentin extended an envelope to me.

"I don't want nothing from you."

"It's not from me. It's a letter Ms. Duncan left for

you. Ricky said you never came by to pick it up, and he wanted to give it to you."

I snatched the envelope from Quentin and stormed off with Supreme, refusing to bring any added stress on myself. I had to stay strong and focused for Aaliyah. I would figure out how to deal with Quentin Jacobs after Supreme and I got over this hurdle with our daughter.

When I sat down, I thought back to the funeral and Ricky telling me that Ms. Duncan had left something for me. Nico and I had to rush back to Philly, so I never had a chance to stop by her house and pick it up. With so much drama going on, I had honestly forgotten. I opened the envelope to what were the last words Ms. Duncan wanted me to hear from her.

Dear Precious:

As you read this letter, please know that I'm now at peace and in a better place. When I found out I had cancer, I cried every day and night for over a week. The doctor told me it was too late to get any treatment, and that I was going to die. Those words cut me like a knife. I didn't want to die. I felt like only in the last couple of years I had truly began to live and appreciate life, and to now have it taken from me was a heartbreaking reality. But once I prayed about it, had several conversations with God and accepted it, I then began a new journey in my life. I wanted to free myself of secrets that had been so heavy in my heart. And that's why I'm writing this letter to you.

Precious, you know you were always special to me. As feisty as you was, I could always see that sparkle in your eyes, a sweetness and gentleness that you rarely revealed. I knew a lot of that had to do with all the struggles you had to endure at such a young age. But you've grown to be such a beautiful woman, and I'm so proud of you. Please believe that.

And now you have your own family, and you know how important it is for a child to have both their mother and father in their lives. I truly believe that a great deal of your pain came from never knowing who your father was. And that's why I've decided to tell you. I know you're grown now, but I have to believe that the saying, "Better late than never" applies here.

Your mother knew he was your daddy, but for her own personal reasons, she never wanted him or you to know. Unfortunately, she's no longer here to answer any of those questions, but your father is very much alive. After reading this letter, if you decide you want him to be a part of your life, my brother, Ricky knows how to contact him. Your father is a man named Quentin Jacobs. If you ever want to understand who you are, talk to that man, because he is truly one of a kind, just like you.

Love Always,

Ms. Duncan

Before I could even let myself go through the emotions of what I was feeling after reading Ms. Duncan's letter, I saw Dr. Katz approaching.

"Mr. and Mrs. Mills," Dr. Katz said, keeping his voiced composed.

"How is she?" both me and Supreme asked at the same time.

"We were able to stabilize your daughter, but she's still in critical condition. Aaliyah has lost a massive amount of blood and is going to need a blood transfusion."

I swallowed hard as my heart sank, realizing that even though the surgery went fine, Aaliyah wasn't in the clear yet. I saw Nico, Genesis and Quentin walk near us so they could hear what Dr. Katz was saying. Having Genesis and Nico by my side did seem to give me more strength, and I totally needed it.

"So what's next, Doctor?" Supreme questioned.

"I'm going to be very straight with you. African American Blacks in the United States have a disproportionately large number of individuals with rare blood types unique to race. Those who need a blood transfusion require an exact match of certain blood traits with their own, statistically, because these traits are inherited. A patient's most likely match is another family member. Unfortunately, over seventy-percent of African American Blacks can not find a blood type within their own family. The reason I gave you the long-winded background information on this is because not only does your daughter have those odds working against her, but she also has a rare blood type of AB-negative. Do either one of you know your blood type?"

"I don't," I stated.

"Neither do I," Supreme admitted too.

"We can perform a test and get that information very quickly. But just in case neither one of you are a match, we've already begun searching our database, but I would recommend you contact any family members who might be a match. Your daughter's life depends on it."

"Take the blood test, do whatever you have to do because my daughter will survive. I put that on everything I love," I promised...

Epilogue

The Future

Aaliyah

"Hi!" I waved at the security guard as I entered the palatial estate. I then blew him a kiss and a flirtatious wink. I couldn't help myself, he was outrageously sexy. I knew the shit made him uncomfortable, because he knew my dad would have his ass even though he wasn't doing anything wrong. It was all me. But my dad wouldn't care. In his eyes, his precious Aaliyah could do no wrong.

I parked the new sports car my dad got me for my birthday behind one of his fleet of vehicles. He had the silver drop top specially designed to my liking, and I adored him for it. "Where is my daddy?" I asked one of the maids when I walked in.

"He's in his office, Ms. Aaliayah."

"Thanks, Maria. And would you prepare my lunch? I'll be eating outside by the pool."

"Of course, Ms. Aaliayah."

I gave her a gracious smile and hurried off to see my dad.

"Daddy!" I started calling out before even making it down the hallway. I always did that. It was my way of preparing him for my arrival. When I got to his office, the door was open and he was sitting behind his desk, wrapping up a phone conversation.

"There's my princess!" he said, coming from behind his desk to give me a hug. "How's your day been going?"

"I went to the spa and got a manicure and pedicure. You know, the typical stuff I do during the summer when school is out. But I better enjoy it while I can, since school starts back in a couple of weeks. This summer flew by. Hold up, let me get that. It's Mom calling," I said, answering my cell. "Hey, Mother, what's going on?"

"Just checking up on you. What are you doing?"

"Standing here talking to Daddy."

"Put your father on the phone. I need to ask him something."

"Mom wants to speak to you," I said, handing him my cell.

"Precious, how are you?"

"Good, and you?"

"Everything is going very well."

"That's good to hear, but I wouldn't expect anything different."

"So, what can I do for you?"

"We're having a huge back to school party for Aaliyah and all her classmates, since it's her senior year. I wanted to see if you would be able to attend. You know how much she would enjoy that."

"How would your husband feel?"

"Nico, don't start. You know Supreme would want Aaliyah to be happy, and you being there would do that, so he's fine with it."

"Just asking. Didn't want to ruin Aaliyah's party because Supreme would have a problem with me being there."

"Must we have this conversation every time I speak with you? Supreme accepted years ago that you're Aaliyah's biological dad, but he is also a father to her too. So, I'll see you next month."

"Precious, how are you really?"

"Nico, I have to go."

"You haven't answered my question."

"We agreed not to do this anymore. And you wonder why Supreme has a problem with you. It has nothing to do with your relationship with Aaliyah, it's because he feels *we're* still in a relationship."

"We are. It is called 'co-parenting'."

"Goodbye, Nico. Enjoy the rest of the summer with your daughter."

"Mother didn't have anything else to say to me?" I questioned, taking my phone from my dad.

"No, she had to take another call, but she said she'll call you back later on." Before I could find out why my mother ended her call so abruptly I got a pleasant surprise.

"How's my favorite niece?"

"Uncle Genesis, I didn't even know you were here!" I smiled, giving him a hug. "Did Amir come with you?"

"Yes, he's out by the pool."

"I have so much to talk to him about. I'll see you both later. Bye, Daddy. Bye, Uncle Genesis." I gave them my signature rich-girl-next-door smile, and rushed off to find Amir.

Uncle Genesis was like an uncle to me, but Amir definitely wasn't like a cousin. He was way too stunning for me to ever put him in that category. He was the spitting image of his daddy, and every time I laid eyes on him, I was thankful we weren't related by blood, only by association. Unfortunately, Amir didn't see it that way. But I considered that to be a small obstacle, nothing to stress over too much. I mean, with every passing month I was blossoming more and more into a certified banger. There was only so much self-control any young, hormone crazy, boy could have. Eventually, I would catch Amir at a weak moment, and whisper the right thing in hs ear. Then, all that "we're cousins" shit would be out the window.

"Amir, baby, what is up?" I greeted him, extra

bubbly and interrupting him in the middle of some text message he was typing.

"What's good with you?"

"A whole lot. I have a proposition for you. Are you down for making a lot of money?"

"Aaliyah, what are you talking about? We have money and a lot of it."

"No, our fathers' have a lot of money. I think it's time we start making our own. Are you in or what?"

"Like my father always says, when people come to him with a business proposition, speak…make me want to open my wallet."

"Well, baby, I'm not asking you to open your wallet. You follow my rules, I guarantee you, I'ma put money in it."

Once I gave Amir my signature rich-girl-next-door smile, I knew I would close the deal.

Bitch . . .
A New Beginning
COMING 2011

COMING SOON!

Trife Life To Lavish

Part 2

Genesis & Genevieve...Am I My Brother's Keeper

IN STORES NOW

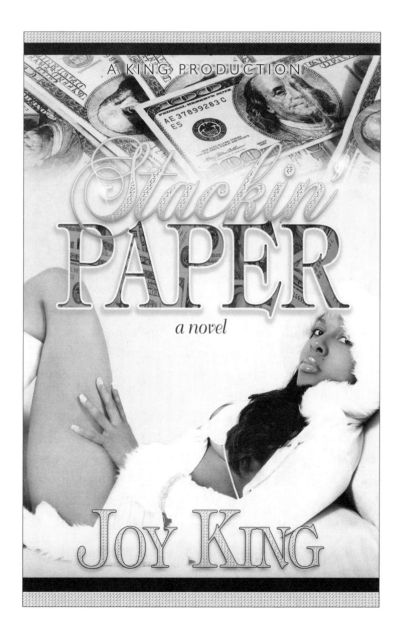

A KING PRODUCTION

Stackin'
PAPER

a novel

JOY KING

Chapter One
A Killer Is Born

Philly, 1993

"Please, Daquan, don't hit me again!" the young mother screamed, covering her face in defense mode. She hurriedly pushed herself away from her predator, sliding her body on the cold hardwood floor.

"Bitch, get yo' ass back over here!" he barked, grabbing her matted black hair and dragging her into the kitchen. He reached for the hot skillet from the top of the oven, and you could hear the oil popping underneath the fried chicken his wife had been cooking right before he came home. "Didn't I tell you to have my food ready on the table when I came home?"

"I... I... I was almost finished, but you came home early," Teresa stuttered, "Ouch!" she yelled as her neck damn near snapped when Daquan gripped her hair even tighter.

"I don't want to hear your fuckin' excuses. That's what yo' problem is. You so damn hard headed and neva want to listen. But like they say, a hard head make fo' a soft ass. You gon' learn to listen to me."

"Please, please, Daquan, don't do this! Let me finish frying your chicken and I'll never do this again. Your food will be ready and on the table everyday on time. I promise!"

"I'm tired of hearing your damn excuses."

"Bang!" was all you heard as the hot skillet came crashing down on Teresa's head. The hot oil splashed up in the air, and if Daquan hadn't moved forward and turned his head, his face would've been saturated with the grease. But Teresa wasn't so lucky, as the burning oil grazed her hands, as they were protecting her face and part of her thigh.

After belting out in pain from the grease, she then noticed blood trickling down from the open gash on the side of her forehead. But it didn't stop there. Daquan then put the skillet down and began kicking Teresa in her ribs and back like she was a diseased infected dog that had just bitten him.

"Yo', Pops, leave moms alone! Why you always got to do this? It ain't never no peace when you come in this house." Genesis stood in the kitchen entrance with his fists clenched and panting like a bull. He had grown sick and tired of watching his father beat his mother down almost every single day. At the age of eleven he had seen his mother receive more ass whippings than hugs or any indication of love.

"Boy, who the fuck you talkin' to? You betta get yo' ass back in your room and stay the hell outta of grown people's business."

"Genesis, listen to your father. I'll be alright. Now go back to your room," his mother pleaded.

Genesis just stood there unable to move, watching his mother and feeling helpless. The blood was now covering her white nightgown and she was covering her midsection, obviously in pain trying to protect the baby that was growing inside of her. He was in a trance, not knowing what to do to make the madness stop. But he was quickly brought back to reality when he felt his jaw almost crack from the punch his father landed on the side of his face.

"I ain't gon' tell you again. Get yo' ass back in your room! And don't come out until I tell you to! Now go!" Daquan didn't even wait to let his only son go back to his room. He immediately went over to Teresa and picked up where he left off, punishing her body with punches and kicks. He seemed oblivious to the fact that not only was he killing her, but also he was killing his unborn child right before his son's eyes.

A tear streamed down Genesis's face as he tried to reflect on one happy time he had with his dad, but he went blank. There were no happy times. From the first moment he could remember, his dad was a monster.

All Genesis remembered starting from the age of three was the constant beat downs his mother endured for no reason. If his dad's clothes weren't ironed just right, then a blow to the face. If the volume of the television was too loud, then a jab here. And, God forbid, if the small, two-bedroom apartment in the drug-infested building they lived in wasn't spotless, a nuclear bomb would explode in the form of Daquan. But the crazy part was, no matter how clean their apartment was or how good the food was cooked and his clothes being ironed just right, it was never good enough. Daquan would bust in the door, drunk or high, full of anger, ready to take out all his frustration out on his wife. The dead end jobs, being broke, living in the drug infested and violent prone city of Philadelphia had turned the already troubled man into poison to his whole family.

"Daddy, leave my mom alone," Genesis said in a calm, unemotional tone. Daquan kept striking Teresa as if he didn't hear his son. "I'm not gonna to tell you again. Leave my mom alone." This time Daquan heard his son's warning but seemed unfazed.

"I guess that swollen jaw wasn't enough for you. You dying to get that ass beat." Daquan looked down at a now black and blue Teresa who seemed to be about to take her last breath. "You keep yo' ass right here, while I teach our son a lesson." Teresa reached her hand out with the little strength she had left trying to save her son. But she quickly realized it was too late. The sins of the parents had now falling upon their child.

"Get away from my mother. I want you to leave and don't ever come back."

Daquan was so caught up in the lashing he had been putting on his wife that he didn't even notice Genesis retrieving the gun he left on the kitchen counter until he had it raised and pointed in his direction. "Lil' fuck, you un lost yo' damn mind! You gon' make me beat you with the tip of my gun."

Daquan reached his hand out to grab the gun out of Genesis's hand, and when he moved his leg forward, it would be the last step he'd ever take in his life. The single shot fired ripped through Daquan's heart and he collapsed on the kitchen floor, dying instantly.

Genesis was frozen and his mother began crying hysterically.

"Oh dear God!" Teresa moaned, trying to gasp for air. "Oh, Genesis baby, what have you done?" She stared at Daquan, who laid face up with his eyes wide open in shock. He died not believing until it was too late that his own son would be the one to take him out this world.

It wasn't until they heard the pounding on the front door that Genesis snapped back to the severity of the situation at hand.

"Is everything alright in there?" they heard the older lady from across the hall ask.

Genesis walked to the door still gripping the .380-caliber semi-automatic. He opened the door and said in a serene voice, "No, Ms. Johnson, everything is *not* alright. I just killed my father."

Two months later, Teresa cried as she watched her son being taking away to spend a minimum of two years in a juvenile facility in Pemberton, New Jersey.

Although it was obvious by the bruises on both Teresa and Genesis that he acted in self defense, the judge felt that the young boy having to live with the guilt of murdering his own father wasn't punishment enough. He concluded that if Genesis didn't get a hard wake up call, he would be headed on a path of self destruction. He first ordered him to stay at the juvenile facility until he was eighteen. But after pleas from his mother, neighbors and his teacher, who testified that Genesis had the ability to accomplish whatever he wanted in life because of how smart and gifted he was, the judge reduced it to two years, but only if he demonstrated excellent behavior during his time there. Those two years turned into four and four turned into seven. At the age of eighteen when Genesis was finally released he was no longer a young boy, he was now a criminal minded man.

IN STORES NOW

A KING PRODUCTION

Trife Life To Lavish

DEJA KING

Prologue
Escaping the Madness
Charlotte, North Carolina The Past...

"Get the fuck outta my house!" Teresa screamed, as she stood in the entrance of the bedroom door. Teresa's initial reaction was to drag the woman lying on her back out of the bed, but seeing the horrific shock on the woman's face made her quickly reassess that decision. Teresa and the other woman both seemed to be stuck on pause, and the only person being on fast forward was the man who continued getting his stroke on as if nothing was going to stop him from busting a nutt.

"Oh shit! I'm almost there!" the man moaned, speeding up his pace as if oblivious to the fact that he had a viewing audience.

Teresa couldn't believe she was watching as her husband fucked another woman right in front of her face. Immediately, flashback images consumed her. She thought back to all the bullshit she had been enduring for the last six years.

In the beginning, Kevon seemed to be Teresa's saving grace. She had a baby girl, who was just over a year old, had no money, no job and a bleak future. The landlord had given her an eviction notice, and Teresa was going to have to go live with her mother so she and her baby wouldn't be homeless. But that never happened, because Kevon swooped in and took on the role as her man, and a father to her daughter, Genevieve. Teresa was so enamored, that when Kevon asked that she and the baby come back to live with him at his crib in Charlotte, she packed up and left Philly, the only place she had ever called home.

Teresa felt like she had died and gone to suburban heaven, when she first arrived at the handsome two-story brick house on the tree-lined street. She had grown accustomed to living in drug infested project buildings with hallways smelling like piss, and where trash replaced grass as landscaping. Inhaling the fresh, clean air in the south seemed like a life she would only daydream about, not actually live.

But Teresa's daydreaming quickly turned into a

never-ending nightmare after marrying Kevon. He was no longer her saving grace, but instead the cause of her demise.

"What the fuck is you doing here? I thought you wasn't gonna be home for another hour," Kevon spit, after finally busting a nutt and pulling himself out of the stiffened woman.

Teresa's mind was so far gone with reflecting on the horrors of the past, that at first she didn't hear her husband.

"Bitch, don't you hear me talking to you?" Kevon continued.

"Nigga, fuck you!" Teresa barked, coming out her daze. "You so damn trifling, you gon' bring another woman in my house and fuck her in my bed? I'm so sick of your disrespectful bullshit, I don't know what to do!"

"I swear I had no idea he was married, or that this was your home!" the fear stricken girl who looked no more than eighteen said, pleading her case to Teresa. She jumped out of bed, scrambling to get her clothes on, in an attempt to escape without the ass whooping she assumed his wife was about to put on her.

But unbeknownst to the teeny bopper, Teresa was beginning to grow so immune to her husband's revolting behavior, that she refused to waste her energy on beating any of his women down. Plus, she believed the girl when she said she was clueless to Kevon's marital status. This here situation needed to be handled with one person—her husband.

"You ain't got to explain shit to her! This *my* house. It ain't my fault she brought her ass back home early."

Teresa stood with her eyes twitching. *This nigga is determined to have a throw-down up in this mutherfucka, and I'ma give it to him!* "Little girl, I think it's best you go. I need to deal with my husband."

The girl nodded her head in agreement with Teresa's request, and leaped up to make an exit.

"I'll call you later on," Kevon said, casually, making it clear he wasn't pressed about how pissed Teresa was.

"Ma, who was that woman that just ran up out of here?"

Teresa looked down at her seven-year-old daughter. With all the anger consuming her, she had forgotten she was there. "Genevieve, baby, she was nobody. You go to your bedroom and close the door. I got some things to handle with your father."

Genevieve looked over at her father as he stood in only his boxer shorts, before asking, "Daddy, is everything okay?"

"I'm good," he answered, pulling out a box of cigarettes from his pants pocket and grabbing a pack of matches off the dresser to light up.

"Genevieve, g'on to your room and color or

something. I'll be there in a minute."

"But I'm hungry."

Teresa slit her eyes at her daughter, not in the mood for no whining. "I'ma tell you one more time to go to your room," Teresa said, in a threatening tone that Genevieve knew all too well. "I'ma make you something to eat when I'm done in here. Now g'on!"

Genevieve looked back at her daddy, then her mom, before walking out their room. But instead of going to her bedroom like she was told, she sat down in the hallway corner, determined to find out what had her mother so angry.

"Teresa, I don't feel like hearing whateva bullshit 'bout to come out yo' mouth," Kevon said, slipping on his jeans.

"You should'a thought about that before you brought some young ass girl up in this house!"

"Oh, would it make you feel better if I would'a brought some old ass woman up in here to fuck? I mean, I'm just saying…"

"You know what, Kevon? Why don't you pack up your shit and get the fuck out. Clearly this ain't where you wanna be no more, so I think it's best you leave."

Kevon gave a low chuckle before taking a pull off the cigarette and laying it down in the ashtray. "I hope you ain't been dabbling in my stash, because only some powerful yang can have you speaking out the side of your neck like that. 'Cause I ain't going no motherfuckin' where."

"Well, you won't be staying up in here with me with this disrespectful bullshit. I'm tired, Kevon. From you getting other bitches pregnant, having ho's stashed up in apartments, to them blowing up my phone looking for you. Now, you so sloppy wit' yo' shit, you bringing broads to the place I lay my head. I can't live like this! I won't live like this!"

"Bitch, have you forgotten where I found your busted ass at? You was a broke-down ho, with not even one dollar to your name. You didn't even have enough money to buy milk or pampers for your baby. If it wasn't for me, you and Genevieve would still be in Philly, struggling just to get by. So save all that 'you can't live like this'. You better be happy you gotta place to live."

"Oh really? You don't want to leave? Then I'll leave, 'cause anything is better than this." Teresa turned to walk away, facing the fact that she was fighting a useless cause.

"Where the fuck you think you going?" Kevon yanked Teresa's arm, stopping her from walking away.

"Get the fuck off of me! I told you I'm done wit' this shit."

"Nah, we ain't done until I say we done. I been taking care of you and a child that ain't even mine, and you think you gon' just leave me? You fuckin' crazy! That's not how this shit work. I pulled you out of those projects and made an honest woman outta you, so you owe me your life just for that."

"I don't owe you shit! And if I did, I've paid my debt in full having to deal wit' all your drama over the years. Now, get the fuck off of me! I'm taking my daughter and getting the fuck outta here."

The next thing Teresa knew, she was hitting the floor from the impact of the punch Kevon landed on her face. *This nigga been cheating on me for all these years, now he wanna put his hands on me too! Aahh, hell no!* Teresa thought as she lay on the floor staring up at the man she once believed was the best thing that ever happened to her.

"You see what you made me do? I've been nothing but a provider for you and Genevieve, and this is the respect I get. That's why you gotta treat women like hos and tricks, 'cause ya' don't 'preciate nothing. But you my wife, and you will respect me."

"Kevon, get away from me! I promised myself I would neva let another man put their hands on me, and I meant that shit!"

Kevon grabbed Teresa by her hair and dragged her over near the dresser. Teresa was swinging her arms and kicking her legs, irate and scared, not knowing what Kevon was going to do next. But Kevon was undeterred.

"You think you gon' talk shit to me in my house

where I pay the bills? I don't give a fuck if you caught me up in this crib everyday wit' a different bitch, you show me respect. But just like you gotta beat obedience in your children, I'ma put the fear of God in you," he said, grabbing the still lit cigarette from the ashtray.

"Kevon, no-o-o-o-o-o!" Teresa screamed out as little pieces of ashes were falling down, barely missing her exposed skin.

"Ain't no use in screaming now. You should'a thought about that shit before running off at the mouth." Kevon lifted Teresa up off the floor like a rag doll. Her petite frame dangled in the air as Kevon pointed the cigarette towards her face. "Now, where shall I leave my mark? Some place where you can constantly look at, as a reminder that you'll always be my bitch."

All anyone could hear were the gut wrenching cries of pain as Kevon mashed the cigarette into the upper right side of Teresa's left breast.

Before he released her hair and Teresa dropped to the floor, she caught a glimpse of the devilish smirk on Kevon's face. The pain was overwhelmingly excruciating, but seeing the gratified look on her husband's mug as he was leaving her there to suffer gave Teresa the strength to fight back. With his back turned, believing she was in no condition to defend herself, Teresa grabbed the marble lamp off the nightstand, and with all her might, slammed it over Kevon's head, not once, not twice, but three times.

Exhausted from using all her strength, Teresa let the lamp drop out of her hands, and when she looked up, she saw her daughter, Genevieve standing only feet away with a blank stare on her face. Teresa then looked down at Kevon, and blood was pouring from the open gash on his head.

"Oh shit, he's dead!" Teresa mumbled, as she shook his rigid body, looking for any sign of life.

"Ma, is Daddy dead? Did you kill Daddy?"

"This man here, ain't none of your Daddy," Teresa said, firmly latching onto her daughter's arm.

Genevieve's eyes filled with tears. She heard the harsh words exchanged between her parents, but didn't want to believe they were true. Kevon was the only father she'd known, and although he didn't treat her mother well all the time, for the most part, he had been decent towards her. But now her mother was affirming the worst; Kevon wasn't her father, and now he was dead.

"I can't believe you killed my Daddy!" Genevieve said, under sniffles, still unable to call him anything else.

"Didn't you hear what I said? That man ain't none of your Daddy!" Teresa screamed, pointing to the dead body. "Now hush up with that crying! I need to think." Teresa's hands were shaking and her head throbbing. She wanted to get away from Kevon and leave him with some of the pain he had caused her, but murder was never part of the equation.

"Ma, what you gon' do?"

"You mean what *we* gon' do? We getting the hell outta here. Go to your room and pack up as much stuff you can fit in here," Teresa ordered, opening the closet door and handing her daughter a suitcase.

"But I don't wanna leave Daddy like this!" The tears were now flowing down Genevieve's face.

"Look at me. I said, look at me!" Teresa yelled, holding her daughter tightly. She knelt down on the floor so she could be eye level with Genevieve. "I know you scared, baby, so am I. But mommy had to defend herself. I didn't mean to kill Kevon, it was an accident, but the police probably wouldn't believe me. I would go to jail and they would send you away to some foster home. I don't want to lose you, baby, so we have to leave."

"And go where, Ma?"

"I'm not sure, but somewhere far away, where nobody knows us or can find us. All we have is each other now, so please, baby, don't fight me. Do what Mommy says. Go to your room and pack up your things. I'll come get you when it's time to go."

Genevieve looked over at Kevon and back into the eyes of her mother. She grabbed the suitcase and left the room.

Teresa wanted to break down and cry, not to mourn the death of her husband, but because she knew her life would never be the same again. She spent the next hour packing up her belongings and trashing the place. When Kevon's body was discovered, she hoped that it would appear as if someone had broken in looking for either money or drugs. It was known in the streets of Charlotte that Kevon was heavily involved with the drug game, and other illegal activities.

Before Teresa left, she grabbed the murder weapon and wrapped it up in a towel before putting it in one of her bags. She then went to Kevon's closet and took the money he always kept in a pair of Timberland boots. She knew Kevon had another spot where he stashed his drugs and real paper, but had no idea exactly where it was, nor did she have the time to try and figure it out. The money Teresa took wasn't enough to ball, but it would hold them over until they found a new home.

"Genevieve, it's time to go, baby," Teresa said, calmly. She held her daughter's hand and looked around the place she'd called home for years. Not only would their lives change, but so would their names. Teresa and Genevieve no longer existed, she decided, closing the door and escaping the madness.

IN STORES NOW

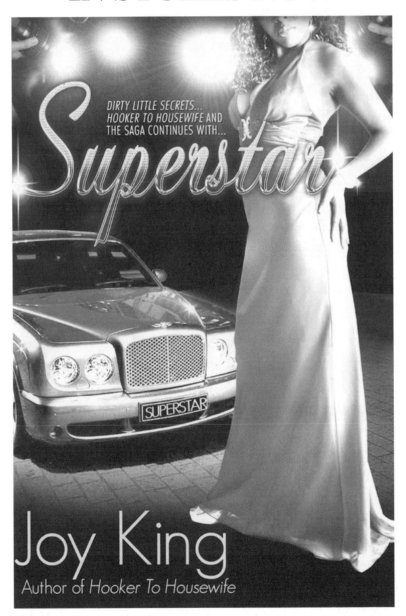

DIRTY LITTLE SECRETS...
HOOKER TO HOUSEWIFE AND
THE SAGA CONTINUES WITH...

Superstar

SUPERSTAR

Joy King

Author of *Hooker To Housewife*

hooker to housewife

Sweet Dreams

Chantal was standing in the building that represented her new future. Everything that happened in the past was of no consequence. Today was the beginning of the rest of her life. Growing up in the projects of Southside Chicago, where she stood right now was said to be the impossible. There always seemed to be limits put upon her dreams. While most of her homegirls' biggest ambitions were to date the local drug dealer, Chantal had always wanted more. She came into the world believing she was special and deserved the best in life. When her friends would brag about a new pair of shoes some guy bought them, Chantal felt a guy should buy her the whole store. It wasn't just because she was the prettiest girl in her neighborhood and school, but she was more beautiful than any star on television and she didn't have their money to buy the illusion. Her beauty was God-given and her mother always told her how blessed she was. She stressed the importance of not using her looks for evil, which she considered to be for selfish material gain. That never sat right with Chantal; she often said to her mother, "What was the sense of God blessing me with such a gorgeous face and body if I can't use it to my advantage?"

Chantal thought back to how her mother read the bible every morning at the breakfast table. Up until the very end, Mrs. Morgan continued to try and instill morals into her willful daughter. She would bribe Chantal to go to church every Sunday by promising her a new outfit or buying her something that she knew they couldn't afford. But one day that was no longer enough for Chantal and she ended that abruptly. Mrs. Morgan knocked on Chantal's bedroom door and she was just lying in bed staring at the wall. First her mother thought she wasn't feeling well until Chantal said, "Why should I waste my time and best clothes to go to a place where I'll never meet my husband. Plus people that go to church are the biggest sinners anyway." With that, Chantal put the covers over her face and waited for her mother to close the door. From that day on Chantal went into full-blown rebellion.

Chantal had made it clear to her parents that her

sole goal in life was to marry a rich powerful man who would spoil her like the star she was supposed to be. She was tired of seeing her parents struggle all their lives barely making ends meet. It seemed like yesterday that she was sitting on the school bus admiring a picture of a very wealthy mogul whose face was splashed across the front cover of a magazine with the headline KING OF NEW YORK. That photo and inside story was her motivation to leave the hood behind and seek the jet-set life she craved.

The road Chantal traveled to get here definitely wasn't an easy one. When she arrived in New York with the $7,000 she stole from her mother, she soon realized that would only get her so far. After renting a hole in the wall room on a weekly basis she immediately started hitting the club scene in the heart of the city. One night while seductively gyrating in the middle of the dance floor she caught the eye of a well-known video music director. He promised that if she listened to his advice he would make her a music video queen. Even then Chantal thought prancing around in videos was beneath her, but she knew it would get her within touching distance of all the music bigwigs. In her mind she felt that was all she needed; once the music industry honchos got an eyeful of her, one of them was bound to put a huge rock on her finger. The next day she called the director and he kept his word. Now seven years later she was about to marry the most powerful man in the music industry. Who said that dreams never come true?

"Chantal, I can't believe today is the big day! Girl I'm about to start crying like I'm getting married," Shari said under sniffles, bringing Chantal out of her deep thoughts of the past.

"Shari, this has to be the happiest day of my life. All my dreams are about to come true. If someone would have told me ten years ago that I would be getting married at a church on Rodeo Drive in Beverly Hills I would've burst out laughing, but look at me. Today that is exactly what is about to happen. I have my best friend by my side, my beautiful little girl, and the man I love. My parents might have thought I was a major screw-up but I've made them proud. I've landed the biggest catch of them all."

"Yeah you have," Shari nodded in agreement. Both women looked around at the thousands of flowers and the beautifully decorated church. It was of the caliber to make even Star Jones second-guess her wedding planner. "Listen, Cinderella, it's time for us to get you dressed and ready for the momentous occasion. In a couple of hours this church will be filled to capacity and it will be your moment to shine.

Kenny entered Andre's house close to ten o'clock in the morning still replaying his late-night rendezvous with two buxom twins. Although they wanted to keep the party going, and so did he, Kenny was determined to be at his best friend's side for his wedding day. Right when he was about to skip up the stairs and take a quick shower he was startled when he saw what looked like two bodies wrapped around each other in the living room. As he walked closer, trying to focus on the image, he felt an arousal at the outline of a woman's glistening body peeking from the blanket. He still couldn't see her face but soon realized that the well-defined man's body was no other than Andre's. Kenny couldn't help but say out loud, "That's my man. You decided to get some before taking the plunge." Kenny's thunderous mouth instantly woke up Andre and he saw that Tyler was still sleep.

"Man, keep it down!" Andre demanded, while making sure the blanket covered Tyler's naked body, and he grabbed his boxer shorts.

"Who is that?" Kenny asked, trying to get a better view of the sleeping woman. Andre grabbed Kenny's arm and led him into his study. Andre didn't say another word until they reached the destination and he closed the door behind them. "Man, you still didn't answer my question. Who is that fine piece of ass lying on your living room floor?" Andre gave Kenny an intense glare that sent chills down his spine. "Did I say something wrong?" Kenny said, feeling uncomfortable with the look Andre was giving him.

"That woman you're talking about is my future wife."

"What? I know the pussy might have been good but damn, man. Your future wife is waiting for you at the church." Andre wanted to punch Kenny in his mouth because he felt as if he was disrespecting Tyler in some way, but then he also knew that Kenny thought the woman in his living room was just some random chick.

"Listen, Kenny, that woman in the living room is Tyler."

"Tyler Blake the movie star? Stop playing, man." Kenny made a gesture as if he was about to leave the study and go back to the living room to drool over the sleeping starlet.

"Where the fuck do you think you're going?" Andre asked, stunned by Kenny's actions.

"I have to go see for myself. There is no way that Tyler Blake is lying on your living room floor butt-ass naked." Andre grabbed Kenny's arm with serious intent.

"Man, if you don't stop saying her name in the same sentence as some disrespectable shit we gon have a problem. No my fault, you're going to have a problem," he warned.

"My bad—I didn't realize. I'm just so amped right now. I know you said you dated her but I must have never told you that I have a crush on her." Andre rolled his eyes and started shaking his head, not believing that his childhood best friend was acting like a straight up groupie right now.

"I more than dated her, Kenny. If you get your head out your ass you'll remember that just last night I told you I had asked her to marry me."

"Yeah, you did tell me that. I guess I had selected amnesia. Now I can't even fantasize about her no more. So what now, you guys are back together? When did all this happen?"

"It's a long complicated story, but the point is we're in love and we're getting married."

"What about Chantal? You know I'm not a big fan of hers but man she is going to be devastated."

"I know, and Melanie she's going to take it really hard. But I have the chance to be with the woman I truly love. This is the rest of my life we're talking about." Andre sat on top of his cherry wood desk and stared at the picture of him with Chantal and Melanie. They did look picture-perfect but his heart wasn't there; it belonged to Tyler. Deep down inside, Andre believed in the future he could make Melanie understand that she would always be his angel but things just didn't work out between her parents.

"I totally understand. I didn't think you should've gotten engaged to Chantal in the first place. The timing is just so bad. You actually are going to leave that girl at the altar?"

"I'm so torn right now, Kenny, but I do know I won't be marrying Chantal today or any other day. I need to ask you to do me a favor and step up to the plate."

"Hell no! Don't even ask me to do what I know your about to say." Kenny had his hands up in defensive mode, waving them, saying, "No."

"Don't make me beg, but I will. Kenny there is no way I can go to that church and confront Chantal. It would hurt her more coming from me. All her friends and family will see me leave and wonder what happened. All the paparazzi that are surrounding the church, it will turn into a circus out there. Please, man, do this for me. I'm going to write a letter that will be here waiting for her when she returns."

"Where are you going?"

"Tyler was supposed to leave for the island of Mystique this morning. I'm going to go with her and we'll take a later flight. By the time Chantal gets here we'll be gone. My letter will fully explain everything. She and Shari can take the trip to Fiji, and hopefully by the time they return, Chantal won't be so angry."

"Andre I don't know, this is the same chick that slit her wrists trying to win you back. She may wig out on me and beat me with her shoe or something."

"Kenny, stop playing," Andre said annoyed by his comment.

"I'm not playing. Something ain't quite right with that chick."

"Listen, go to the church and ask to speak to Chantal in private. Tell her that I sent you because it would hurt too bad to see the disappointment on her face but that I'm not ready to get married. Let her know that I have explained everything in a letter that I left on the nightstand in the bedroom. If she asks where I am, tell her that I got on a flight this morning and would call her later to see how she is doing. But no matter how angry she gets or even if she curses you out, Kenny, do not be cruel to her." Kenny stood in the middle of the study, speechless. He was the same defense attorney who cut prosecution witnesses to shreds on the witness stand, but to have to break the heart of a would-be blushing bride was more than he could stomach.

———————

Chantal stood in the mirror, admiring what a vision of perfection she was. She had never seen a more gorgeous bride. With her full spread layout in *InStyle* magazine she would be the envy of all grown women and little girls everywhere. Chantal's chic chignon hairstyle and super-sized diamond earrings perfectly complemented her white strapless gown that clasped every curve in her hour-glass figure. Chantal's stylist came over and made the final touches to her makeup and it was show time.

"Chantal, are you ready?" Shari asked, as she grabbed her best friend's delicate hand.

"Definitely," Chantal said with pure confidence.

"Before we go out there and you face all those people I want to tell you something. Chantal, I truly love you. You're the sister I never had. To see you standing here looking like a princess is unbelievable. We've been through so much together and I know you truly love Andre and that you're going to make him a wonderful wife. We joke a lot about landing that one sponsor who will change our life forever, but I know you and I know your heart. Andre is the only man that you've ever given your heart to and one day he'll realize just how lucky he is to have a gem like you." The two women held each other in a deep embrace, not noticing that Kenny was standing in the entrance of the door.

"Excuse me, I'm sorry to interrupt but can I speak to Chantal alone for a minute."

"What's up, Kenny? Don't tell me that Andre is running late. Everyone is waiting for us."

"Can I speak to you alone, Chantal?" he repeated, not cracking a smile. Shari could sense that something was wrong but remained unruffled for Chantal.

"Whatever you have to tell me you can say it in front of Shari. She's family."

"I'd much rather tell you in private."

"Chantal, it's not a problem, I'll be right outside," Shari said, making her way to the door.

"No, you stay right here, Shari. I want you to hear what Kenny has to say." Kenny glanced at Shari and then back at Chantal. He so wanted to get the whole thing over with that he wasn't about to go back and forth about if Shari was staying or not. Plus, he figured she would need her girlfriend to console her after the news he was about to break.

"I'm going to come right out with it, Chantal: Andre won't be showing up here today. He can't go through with the wedding," Kenny stated matter-of-factly.

"There must be some mistake. You never liked me, Kenny, and now you're trying to ruin my wedding day. But this isn't funny. There are hundreds of people waiting for me to walk down the isle. Andre would never leave me standing at the altar." The shivering of Chantal's lips and the twitching of what seemed to be her entire face made Shari and Kenny stand there frozen.

"Chantal, calm down. Andre sent me because he didn't' want to see the pain in your face when he broke your heart. He explained everything in a letter that is waiting at home for you."

"A letter, a fucking letter! This isn't happening to me! Andre loves me, he really does. We belong together. No one will ever love Andre the way that I do. He has to marry me. What will I tell Melanie?" Chantal was now sitting on the floor, rocking back and forth. Shari ran to her side and laid her head on Chantal's shoulder, trying to carry some of her pain. At that moment Kenny had not only broken Chantal's heart but Shari's too.

"Chantal, I'm so sorry," Kenny said sincerely.

"Where is he, Kenny? Tell me where Andre is?"

"He took a flight out early this morning. He said he would call you later to make sure you're alright." Before Kenny could say another word, Chantal scurried past him with vengeance in her eyes.

As T-Roc drove down Sunset Boulevard he got the call he'd been waiting for. "Hello. Tell me something good."

"How about I tell you something great," his most trusted informant replied.

"That's even better."

"Meet me at our usual spot in an hour."

"What for, you can't tell me over the phone?"

"The skeleton we hoped to drag out of the closet on your enemy Andre turned out to be a full-fledged grave. This information is so explosive I have to see the expression on your face when I reveal all."

"Say no more. I'm on the way." T-Roc made a U-turn in the middle of the street, smiling at the thought of finally bringing Andre down once and for all.

———————

Tyler finally believed that her heart was at peace. For so long, true love eluded her and she was suppressing the pink inside-out of fear that she would once again be left blindsided by a man's deception. But her love for Andre and his love for her was the key that unlocked all of her inhibitions.

"I can't believe I'm here with you right now. I feel like the luckiest girl in the world," Tyler beamed, as she hugged and kissed Andre.

"You are the luckiest girl and I'm the luckiest guy," he said, rubbing the tip of his nose against the tip of hers. "Although I would love to sit here and debate who is luckier, we need to get dressed and catch this flight. I can't wait to get you on that island and make love to you every day and every night. Not only do I want to make love, but I'm hoping that we'll make a baby. Does that sound like a plan to you?"

"Actually that doesn't sound like a plan at all," Tyler said shifting her body on the couch so her back was now turned away from Andre.

"Tyler, please don't tell me that you want to wait to have kids because of your career? I thought we were past all of that," he said, grabbing her arm so they would be face-to-face. Tyler was trying to hold back the grin that was about to escape, before answering his question.

"No, the reason why we don't have to plan is because we're already pregnant." Tyler stood for a minute absorbing the shocked look on Andre's face. While he sat with his mouth agape she continued, "I knew that when I came over here last night, but I didn't want you to take me back because of a baby. I wanted you to take me back for me, for the love we share for one another."

After finally getting over the initial shock, he said, "You must be at least three months pregnant. I can't believe this. Not only are you going to be my wife but you're also going to be the mother of my child." Andre rubbed Tyler's stomach, overjoyed that he would once again be a father, but this time by a woman he would spend the rest of his life with.

"Andre, this all seems like a dream to me. It's like I don't want to wake up because I'm afraid it won't be real."

"Baby, you don't have to be afraid, this is not a dream. This is about two people who belong together. I promise you that I will spend the rest of my life making you the happiest woman in the world." Andre went in his pants pocket and pulled out the pink diamond engagement ring that Tyler had given back to him what seemed like a lifetime ago. He slid the sparkler on her long slender finger and in both of their hearts they felt like husband and wife.

After making love and then taking a long hot shower and then making love again, the lovebirds were ready to catch their flight to Mystique. Andre and Tyler walked hand-and-hand out the door oblivious to their surroundings because they were so caught up in their love.

Chantal was contaminated with hatred when she bolted out the church and jumped in her Benz. As she sped off, the paparazzi went ballistic coming up with scenarios as to why the bride-to-be stormed out the church like a bat out of hell and where she was off to on her wedding day. Chantal kept replaying the words that Kenny said to her. *Andre isn't going to marry you.* It was suffocating her brain. All she could think about was getting home and reading the letter that he left. There had to be an explanation for all this, and some sort of clue as to how she could get him back. As Chantal pulled up to the driveway she slowed down when she saw what was supposed to have been her future husband lovingly embracing her archenemy. She sat in her car from a distance studying the couple as if they were strangers. The man was standing on the front door steps kissing the woman and running his fingers through her long dark hair. The woman jumped up and wrapped her legs around the man's waist and he twirled her around as if they were new young lovers. They laughed and smiled at one another as if they were the only two people in the world, as if no one else existed or mattered. Chantal couldn't help but wish it was her.

Shari seized Kenny's arm as he was turning to leave. "Wait a minute, Kenny. I want you to tell me what's really going on with Andre."

"No disrespect, Shari, but I explained everything that needed to be said to Chantal. I'm done here."

"How can you come and wreck a woman's world and then say you're done? I know you're not that cold, maybe Andre but not you."

"You don't even know me, so you can't say what type of man I am."

"I know that you were the one who had enough balls to break the news to Chantal, instead of Andre's coward ass doing it."

"I know the whole situation is a little fucked up,

but Andre means well."

"A little! He left the mother of his child at the church on their wedding day. That is more than a little fucked up. Now I have to go out there and explain to hundreds of people and a sweet innocent little girl why her parents aren't getting married today. Now I want some answers." Kenny put his head down and turned his back, leaving Shari to answer her own questions.

Reality returned and Chantal comprehended that the couple weren't strangers but the love of her life Andre and the love of his life, Tyler Blake. She looked down at her $100,000 custom-made Vera Wang wedding gown and the diamond studded Manolo that was placed firmly on the brakes. Her fresh French-manicured hands were gripping the steering wheel to her silver CL600 Coupe. It all made sense now. Andre wasn't marrying her because his heart belonged to a woman that didn't deserve him. No matter how hard Chantal tried, Andre couldn't accept as true that her mentality had gone from hooker to housewife. Instead, he chose a woman that didn't truly love him at all. But there was no way that Tyler Blake would steal her thunder. Andre and Chantal had exchanged vows and it was until death do them part. Chantal lifted one Manolo off the brake and pressed the other on the gas.

Tyler was the first to notice the silver Benz racing toward them. She had a flashback to when she was a teenager in Georgia and everything went in slow motion as Trey, the abusive boyfriend she dated in high school, blew his brains out. Tyler's body once again froze, and as the sound of the engine got closer and louder, Andre slowly turned his head and locked eyes with the deranged Chantal, and all Tyler could let out was, "Andre look out!"

The Saga Continuess...
In Stores Now
Superstar!!

IN STORES NOW

A KING PRODUCTION

Queen BITCH

DEJA KING

Coming Soon!

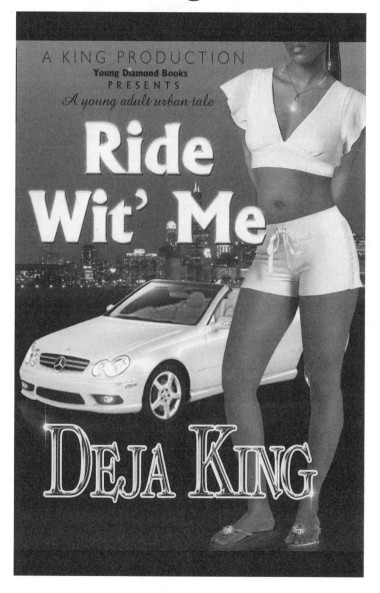

A KING PRODUCTION
Young Diamond Books
PRESENTS
A young adult urban tale

Ride Wit' Me

DEJA KING

A King Production
Order Form

A King Production
P.O. Box 912
Collierville, TN 38027
www.myspace.com/joyking

Name: _____

Address: _____

City/State: _____

Zip: _____

QUANTITY	TITLES	PRICE	TOTAL
____	Bitch	$15.00	_____
____	Bitch Reloaded	$15.00	_____
____	The Bitch Is Back	$15.00	_____
____	Queen Bitch	$15.00	_____
____	Last Bitch Standing	$15.00	_____
____	Dirty Little Secrets	$14.95	_____
____	Hooker to Housewife	$13.95	_____
____	Superstar	$15.00	_____
____	Ride Wit' Me	$12.00	_____
____	Stackin' Paper	$15.00	_____
____	Trife Life To Lavish	$15.00	_____
____	Stackin' Paper II	$15.00	_____

Shipping/Handling (Via Priority Mail) $5.50 1-2 Books, $7.95 3-4 Books add $1.95 for ea. Additional book.

Total: $_____ **FORMS OF ACCEPTED PAYMENTS:** Certified or government issued checks and money Orders, all mail in orders take 5-7 Business days to be delivered.

Joy (Deja) King

About the Author

Deja (Joy) King was born in Toledo, Ohio, and raised in California, Maryland, North Carolina and New Jersey. Ms. King represents a new breed of writers producing young, hip and sexy novels that introduce readers to street life in all its complexity and also takes readers behind the velvet rope of the glamorous, but often shady entertainment industry.

Ms. King attended North Carolina Central University and Pace University, where she majored in journalism. Emerging onto the entertainment scene, Deja accepted an internship position, and immediately began to work her way up the ranks, at The Terrie Williams Agency. She worked hands-on with Johnnie Cochran, The Essence Awards, The Essence Music Festival, The NBA Players' Association, Moet & Chandon, and other entertainment executives and celebrities.

Following a new chapter in her life, Ms. King attended the Lee Strasburg Theater Institute before accepting a job as Director of Hip Hop Artist Relations at Click Radio, where she developed segments featuring the biggest names in hip hop. Ms. King pushed her department to new levels by creating an outlet that placed hip hop in the forefront of the cyber world.

Ms. King made her literary debut with *Bitch*, and followed it up with the bestselling sequel *Bitch Reloaded* and *The Bitch Is Back*. The saga continues with *Queen Bitch*. A prolific writer, King is also the author of *Dirty Little Secrets*, *Hooker to Housewife, Superstar, Stackin' Paper, Trife Life To Lavish* and *Stackin' Paper 2 Genesis' Payback* which she writes under her pseudonym Joy King.

For more information visit www.joykingonline.com and www.myspace.com/joyking.